To Christine

Thanks for visiting

with my

Sanctuary

Susan Bracy
3/29/08

ii

paths of
sanctuary

paths of
sanctuary

a novel by
ihsan bracy

coolgrovepress

all rights reserved under the International and pan-american copyright conventions. published in the united states by cool grove press, an imprint of cool grove publishing, inc., new york.
512 Argyle Road, Brooklyn, NY 11218
http://www.coolgrove.com

Trade Paper: ISBN:
1-887276-49-1   978-1-887276-49-8

acknowledgements

The publication of this book was supported in part by a 2007-8 Face Out re-Grant from the Council of Literary Magazines and Presses [clmp] & the Jerome Foundation. The grant's objective is to raise the profile of an emerging author.

cover art: Rafael Leonardo Black
editor: Celina Davis
book design: Tej Hazarika
cover design assistant: Sage Hazarika
internal support: Candace Hamilton & Islah Sah

also by ihsan bracy
ibo landing: an offering of short stories (cool grove press 1998)
excerpts from *ibo landing* appear in:
new rain vol 9
dark matter
legacy of ibo landing

First edition printed in the United States of America

for jorge and *of course,* for ma

…of empires there shall be seven and the seventh shall stretch from star to star and the greatest… shall be sanctuary…

—from *confessions of a 21st century conjure man*
by arthur flowers

obatala

what's to be done when god has forsaken you, sacrifice or sacrilege? there is no sin that goes unpaid, only deferred. wherefore to turn when there is chaos and confusion, rooted branches of a same fetid tree, in every direction?

attraction and reciprocity feed on the prosperity of death, universal laws provide continuum. chains of memory are nature's profound dna, unraveling secrets within mysteries, sometimes even from beyond the grave.

where can one hide from the wrath of god? ...not even in the eye of a sacred storm.

paths of sanctuary

prologue

1786

twilight spring

summoned by the haunting cries of captured children, a sacred storm silently tracks the stealing prey. at last holding the tiny slave ship firmly within grasp, undiminished ancestral fury rages throughout day and night until on board the slavers know not the difference. retribution has come and once caught there would be no escape, for the storm had hidden the land away from their knowing.

water begins to fill the ship as wood, glue and nail lose to wind's harsh caress. below, the captive lay silent throughout countless hours of labor, all of her life completely given over to this holy task. as the eye of the storm gazes directly overhead there descends a calm and into this silence the captive's screams are fully given. suddenly it is over, the captive pushing forth life from her womb. the afterbirth is soon delivered and birthing completes.

sinking beneath the cold, cold water the captive, in a final act of love, takes off a single strand of tiny irregular shaped blue pearls, her only possession, placing it around her daughter's neck.

suddenly sacrificed into a water world, the scared air bodies are rendered useless. mother ocean's scattered children, shackled and abandoned upon her floor, call out a watery welcome to the newly released souls of their confused brothers and sisters.

floating above the descending mother's submergence, the birthling feeds off the air left within her placenta. she alone heard the silent sirens escorting the slave ship for the last three days, a dolphin pod sensing the onset of labor. the birthling hears more and more dolphins approaching, their sonar beaconed in on a ray so compelling none can turn back.

above, the sacred storm rages relentlessly. beyond, planets realign. below, an older, spotted nurse dolphin moves in and bites through the umbilical cord. the birthling slowly floats to the surface, taking three tiny sips of air before lazily descending. she moves her body in the same fluid motion as dolphins, never removing arms from her side. dolphin mothers and their offspring gently surround the birthling, easily accepting her as one of their own. males form a protective perimeter as the entire convoy turns and heads out to sea.

no one remained to bear witness to a passing sacred storm or remember the sound of its' unbridled ancestral fury.

✳

one

in the path of a-che

just before sunrise the baby is returned unto the shore of angels and into the caressing hands of mother earth. cradled by a gentle lapping of waves, the birthling, color of the red clay which holds her, lies face up into a dawning sky, warmed by the rays of a rising sun.

drawn to the waters' edge by sounds softly lifting from the mud cradle, the white haired spirit-woman finds the birthling closely guarded by a mother dolphin, twin babies by her side, swimming as close as water will allow without beaching. as soon as the birthling is picked up from the waters' edge, the dolphins turn and slowly head back out to join the waiting pod. with the birthling in her arms, the spirit-woman stands and watches, understanding that they have returned this life to shore.

removing the heavy caul that covers her face, the birthling, for the first time, opens her eyes but only whites stare back into the face of spirit. her beautiful brown eyes are turned upward and inward, so consequently she will never see the beauty of this world. the baby holds what seems to be the smallest of smiles and the angel feels a certain peace and calm emanating from the naked child lying in her arms. the child looks fit and she wonders how long the baby has been in the water. long enough, she observes, for the cord to have completely healed and fallen away.

the fat, healthy child must be at least a month old, she concludes. fully intrigued, the spirit-elder understands that the birthling has been fed and cared for by dolphins. now she wonders where the birth mother is or whether she holds dolphin offspring. it is only then that she notices the strand of tiny irregular shaped blue pearls around her neck.

the angel sits playing with the baby on her knee until nearly dusk. questions would arise as to who had really rescued whom on that gentle day. the white haired spirit encloses the birthling in the outer fabric of her blue and white robes and begins walking back toward the village. in all that time the found child does not cry or utter even a sound.

✳

two

in the path of a–che

the red clay path runs from the shore uphill for nearly a quarter of a mile before opening unto a vista revealing the ancient city below. in the distance, salmon colored adobe walls rise alongside connecting red mud footpaths. in this season of fullness the purple skies glow in the warmth of a magenta sunset as spirit-boats return to shore, their white sails slack, their nets full, laden down with the catch of the day, drawn in by evening tides. sunset colors dance off spirit-guides dressed in white garb, gathering in the oncoming dusk. fires lit alongside the shore signal closing off of spirit-passageways as the business of yet another day eases towards its' end.

entering the gates of the spirit-women's compound carrying the infant close to her body, the elderly angel is met by a calling of sacred drums, ringing of ancient bells, the unison of many spirit-women chanting in meditation and the sound of spirit-children hard at play.

not long pass the gates the path divides in two. one way traverses alongside a steep incline, across a shining bridge of fire and runs up towards a white domed clay compound sitting on a cliff overlooking and reflected in the quiet waters of a golden sea below. the other path forks along the compound wall for a short distance before opening onto a sprawling plateau. in between the trees small white mud adobe like structures dot the field of vision as far as the eye could see. as the spirit-woman reaches the yard of her dwelling she is suddenly surrounded by a growing number of spirit-children, fascination clear within their eyes as they silently join the growing and strange procession, clearly watching the bundle she carries with rapt attention. before opening the flap to enter her dwelling, the spirit-elder turns and pulls back her outer robes revealing the foundling to the community. the spirit-children gather around the baby amidst peals of laughter and exhaust their interest before suddenly turning as one and beginning to run downhill, following the path toward the sea.

-blessings of the ancestors upon you nana,

calls out the black, black spirit-sister crossing toward the spirit-elder and the foundling, trailed by a black, black spirit-child not yet six-years-old.

-and upon you too, ntoto

replies the spirit-elder,

-come, look at what mother ocean has given me.

the two spirit-women huddle around the foundling while the spirit-child keeps a distance, his eyes keenly focused on the bundle held just above his head. he doesn't follow all of their conversation but gathers somehow that the baby has been found and doesn't seem to belong to anyone. finally after pulling on his mother's garb twice, she focuses her full attention,

-what is it ladji?

he points until the spirit-elder brings the bundle down to eye level.
he silently studies the foundling with a great intensity before
folding his arms tightly across his near six-year-old chest, proudly
declaring with simple conviction, a big smile and no hesitation,

-this my baby!

after another thought he adds,

-...and we need to call her a-che.

✳

three

in the path of a-che

years pass quickly and true to his word, a-che is rarely found any-where ladji is not. whatever hours daylight sends and what portion of darkness that could be stolen he spends in the company of a-che. it is not unusual to find him sitting outside her hut with the sun-rise and again at sunset, having passed all the time in between in her company. they would walk for hours and through ladji's eyes a-che experiences the colors of the world.

the midday sun's loving arms embrace ladji as he sits cradled with-in the hollow of a large white rock which juts out into golden waters like one of the fingers on a large upturned palm, worn smooth by ocean's constant caress. at the waters' edge sits a-che listening to a pod of gray dolphins which always inhabited waters whenever she is anywhere near a shore. ladji watches her listen and realizes again that a-che is and continues to be a special child. always happy, he could not remember once hearing her cry. as a baby a-che took to water, the element of her birth and would sometimes play there for hours. she could always swim, long before she could walk. nana was the first to notice that whenever a-che came anywhere near water she would see a pod of dolphins in the cove. as soon as a-che entered dolphins would swim as close to her as land allowed. the closer they got the more excited the baby would become pointing and splashing in joy. the dolphins in turn would dive then jump, taking to the air, spinning as a-che would try to leap from nana's arms to swim towards them. nana grasped that dolphin and child were in some kind of constant telepathic communication and again wondered if there was any possible familial connection.

still the color of red mud river clay, a-che is an arrestingly beautiful child with a captivating smile and though her eyes see nothing of the outside world she moves effortlessly around the obstacles of every day life through use of some innate sonar which allows her a certain sort of sight. she senses the placement, shape and density of an object, allowing her freedom to wander without danger of injury and although she rarely speaks, three of a-che's other senses are particularly heightened. with the use of her sonar she could see and track over vast distances under water, she could heal with touch and could sometimes hear the thoughts of any unguarded angel for miles around.

so when ladji approaches her that midday on the beach she already knows what he wants to say.

-tomorrow i must enter the men's compound with
all of the boys of my harvest and if i return, i will be a man.

they both know that once he enters the compound he could be gone for years and that when returned as a man, he would no longer be allowed to meet alone with her. some never return.

ladji and a-che sit there quietly at the waters' edge until well after darkness claims the light of day. slowly returning to nana's hut they part ways long after the evening fires had been lit upon the shores.

✳

four

in the path of a–che

gray, wet skies usher in dawn of a new day. a hush descends over the village as it does every year on the first day of manhood training. the spirit-boys going that year have all snuck away during the night and the village of angels awakens to the emptiness of their silence. as is custom all remain in their perspective compounds to fast, chant and pray for the passage into manhood of the angels in training. a-che feels alone for the first time in her life. ladji had always been there and now he was gone.

years pass before a-che would see him again. ladji stays behind the walls of the compound for more than five years and returns from the house of magic first in his cadre of spirits. in the time that ladji has been gone, a-che has had her own troubles. it has been decided that the baby found and returned by dolphins could not take part in the womanhood rites when her season came. a-che was not of the tribe and therefore could not participate. unless she completed the rites of passage, she would never be considered a woman and consequently could never marry. weighed by an ancient edict which forbids commingling of fire and clay proved to be the encouragement that swayed the final decision of the council of spirit-women.

when ladji returns he is completely distraught upon hearing of the decision. he is turned away when he attempts to see a-che,

-after all,

as nana explains,

-you are now a man and she will always be a child.

there is no perspective that ladji can gain. he has loved a-che from the moment he first laid eyes on her and he loves her still. passage of time does little to diminish ladji's passion. he would see a-che at social functions and sometimes in the village, never alone until late one day, around harvest time when they meet on the path coming back from the well, woven water basket upon her head.

-blessings of the ancestors upon you.

-and upon you too,

she replies, carefully keeping her eyes firmly fixed on the ground at her feet for she does not want to cry.

-are you going tonight?

he refers to the ritual of womanhood passage which her harvest celebrates after nightfall. there was no sound before the almost imperceptible,

-no.

she knows it would be too much to have to wear the white of childhood among the gold and azure of new womanhood.

12

that evening, while the village welcomed the spirit-girls into womanhood, a-che welcomed ladji to her body for what would be the one and only time. afterwards, as a-che lay in the arms of ladji staring into a sky of stars for neither moon showed face, the new lovers plan their future.

-the elders will have to allow us to marry, now...

the number and severity of problems arising from such a suggestion were hard to comprehend. finally the couple decided that it would be easier just to leave, now, while the drums and chants of celebration sounded throughout the village.

a-che begins to get together what few possessions she would carry as ladji goes home to gather his things. the two plan to meet at the bottom of the path below the village. a-che believes she is the first to arrive but destiny patiently lay waiting in a band of captors happening upon the unfortunate, anxious to complete its' karmic mission disrupted nearly twenty years before. sometimes payment for sin is swift and severe, sometimes you're just in the wrong place at the wrong time and sometimes what's coming to you is simply coming to you. either way by the time ladji arrives a-che had been stolen. he waits. at first light he notices tracks of slavers. he follows them to the shore. never again will he feel pain as he does that morning standing, crying on the beach watching a slave ship dancing upon ever distancing waters, carrying a-che and their unknown life away.

✳

silence of passage

five

1865

in the path of dance

that night before was no sleep for any of god's children. up and down the slave row celebratory cries of unexpected laughter continued a spontaneous praise well into the first light of that great gettin' up morning.

dance awakens to find every mouth fondling the new tones of freedom. dance sits up on his pallet of rags and straw to listen. miss mary is singing some song with no intelligible words he can make out other than the occasional,

        -freedom... freedom,

which is punctuated with cries of,

        -thank you, thank you lord jesus!

          -hallelujah!

and

          -praise him!

from other woman as they pass. dance could hear two impassioned voices raised in heated debate directly outside in the dirt lane separating the two rows of slave dwellings. dance stands and throwing off the last vestiges of sleep, slowly walks towards the shaft of light which falls through the open doorway. dance shades his eyes and there stand earl and mason, face-to-face, arguing loudly...

-but where you goin'?

stoically asks mason for the third time,

-just tell me that?

-does it matter? the white hairs in my beard is too many to put number to and never once in 'dis life has i ever set foot off 'dis hateful piece of land.

screams back an animated earl,

-all i know is tonight gonna lay my head down somewhere other than here.

-that's my point, 'xactly...

continues mason,

-just where you goin' ?...

walking around to the ancient tree behind his shack, dance relieves himself as he studies the early summer sky and allows himself for the first time to seriously consider what it would be like to be free. dance knows only one thing for sure, no matter what lie ahead, like earl he would leave today. dance washes in the water trough and as nobody has a mind to cook this morning he prepares a meal of last night's cold cornpone he's saved when suddenly the meeting bell behind the big house begins to ring.

dance stands among the gathered slaves and waits. after a while the screen door slowly opens and out he steps onto the back porch. he removes the ever-present brim, which usually sits upon his head whenever outside and holds it limply in his hand. in stillness the slaves watch as he stands before their silence and for a moment there is no move-ment. dance realizes this is the first time he's ever seen his head and it is completely bald. suddenly he catches a coughing fit, after which he clears his throat again and then again before beginning in a subdued but firm voice to qui-etly speak,

-as of today you are no longer slaves and each
of you is free to go.

there is not a sound heard in response.

-this freedom which shines so brightly is but a false friend
and not to be trusted... you's all welcome to stay on and
work the land as you always has done...

the silence only deepens before he adds,

-for pay.

from the darkening sky a sharp thunderclap seems to reply and give the only answer he would receive. the early summer storm's magnificent arrival on that juneteenth morning signals emancipation for a people and there is an undefined smell of freedom in the rain. drenched in its' downpour, dance, for the first time, walks off the home of his captivity and simply follows the sacred storm.

jubilation unbinds beneath heaven's blanket as dance, cradled in the arms of a large cedar tree, spends his first master-less night counting stars in the safety offered by freedom's canopy under which there were no slaves. later that night freedom, in the form of a five-years-old spirit, gently climbs into the cedar tree where she falls soundly asleep and in love within the arms of the skinny brown-skinned boy she finds there. when morning's birds begin to sing dance opens his eyes to find onyx pools of freedom's light staring deep into his awakening, her eyes silently following his every movement.

as dance went to walk away from the cedar tree she quietly put her little hand in his. she hadn't spoken a word so when he asked her name dance wasn't sure she could even talk. she looks up and softly repeats the only word she has heard that holds any meaning,

-freedom,

and in saying so it became so.

the prospect of living without slavery promises such a sweetness, life's hardships are at first unfathomable. casting their lot on the shoulders of divine destiny with the unwavering belief that its' deliverance must surely provide, the innocent soul and younger spirit set out together to find the mythical north.

*

six

in the path of dance

behold fate the conqueror flatter destiny, the pretender, into believing there is purpose, destination. truth is the destroy-er, uncompromising and unforgiving, relentless and often times the freer of men's souls. the arrival of divinity, hidden beneath the natural order, within time mitigates to a certain extent but there is no getting around the point that, no mat-ter circumstances, the chain of events that bring you to a place on the path was set into vision long before your pre-sent existence. you find yourself simply an aftermath with-in a continuum, where submission comes without choice, quite like the quiet stealth of old age's,

-one day at a time,

culminates in a passage from cradle to grave or similar to the second wave of seed from a long awaited ejaculation, where knowing of its' imminent approach makes you no less powerless to stop it.

it seems everyone was on the move somewhere in this new south, the displaced and the seekers, black and white. the roads were covered with activity. considering dance and freedom's deliverance within the unparalleled context of the

changing times, how two more waifs drifting on emancipation's newly paved highway would eat seemed not much
cause for divine concern and too small a burden for grace's
care. so along with boundless skies and limitless distances,
in the great gettin' up morning the children also discovered
hunger's jagged insides.

survival during the first months of that summer, before
dance learned how to fish, depended on non-ripened fruit,
stolen eggs and milk from farm animals found untended
along their way. the hot days proved long and lazy. with the
coolness of fall the pair scavenge fallen fruit, nuts from abandoned fields, vegetables found in deserted root cellars and
raided clotheslines for extra garments of warmth. they were
always hungry.

around first frost the children come upon a band of about
thirty migrating freed slaves and natives. they decide to
join. it is a new experience living as part of a free collective
and a great comfort to be on the road with others.
there was always plenty of laughter and conversation. dance
realized how much he missed the comfort of other people.
in the daytime the band traveled freely yet freedom was
never found more than a stone's throw from dance. when
they stop at sundown to set up camp the band becomes a
well-oiled machine. there are specific jobs to be done and
soon to the children the routine becomes very familiar.
dance and boys of his age find firewood before dusk and
freedom along with younger girls find the water they always

camped by and carry it back. she likes going for water. it is
the only time that freedom spends totally away from dance.

it had nearly been the same in the evenings on the slave
farm before the grown-folks got back from the fields. there
was order and collectively they watched out for each other,
elders taking care of all the children among them. one took
care of the near child and in doing so prayed somewhere
someone did the same for yours.

there is one tall big-boned woman named reeva who makes
sure freedom's hair is daily combed, dance's shirt washed, his
trousers patched and that somehow they are always fed a
healthy portion of whatever is being,

-et.

dance is intrigued with a native called storm-chaser who
takes him under his wing. storm-chaser teaches him to fish,
use a bow and arrow to hunt small game, to start a fire and
build a shelter both above and below ground.

for the first time in a long while, without hunger's crooked
finger scratching and knawing at their nearly empty insides,
the children sleep soundly next to a fire, surrounded by the
safety and protection of the elders' love. although freedom
lay down with reeva, she never went to sleep until she curled
up next to dance. that was how freedom found him the
night their camp was overrun by marauders terrified by life's
new order and intent on revenge. with bigger game a foot

no one seemed to notice two small children holding hands and slowly backing away, disappearing into night's merciful darkness.

after that dance and freedom stay off the main roads in the daytime, traveling mostly by night. the snow drives the children into a providential cave in which they nearly starve to death while waiting for the cold of winter to kill them. spring's early thaw saves the children. they emerge to find a stream not more than half a mile from the cave's opening filled with fish swimming home. they catch their share and roast them in the ground as storm-chaser had taught dance. that night for the first time in a long while they feast their fill. dance and freedom decide to stay. spending spring and early summer there in relative peace and quiet heal both soul and spirit. it is the happiest period either child would ever remember.

one morning towards the middle of summer dance is sitting at the edge of a pond the children discovered about a mile in the other direction. dance has put out his line and five catfish lay beside him for the trouble. freedom finds some shells and makes up a game which she is playing some twenty feet away. the children, brown from the sun have each gained a slight pouch from their constant source of food. dance lays back and before an insistent nap claims his consciousness the realization hits him that this is his life, freedom-time life. it is proving harder in many ways than slavery-time life but it is his and he was living it. it excites him so much he never does sleep. he celebrates by gleefully gutting catfish. that night after dinner, while watching fireflies, the children once again hear the call of the north. despite this peaceful interlude, dance, recommitted to finding freedom's anticipated rewards, feels it time to strike out and so the tiny spirit and growing soul are once again on the move.

although the desolate pair have traversed many directionless miles in the year of their northern quest, they have never crossed a state line. the children travel mostly at night attempting to keep to themselves but dance had not anticipated the ferocious hunger that reappears to accompany freedom and although he gives her most of what food they find, she always wants more. hunger drives them out from the relative safety of the woods, forcing the children to search out human contact. being half his size and a girl, many times when they come upon an isolated farmhouse, especially if there were women-folk around, dance would hide in the woods to wait for the greater charity which sometime would come freedom's way when she appeared alone.

it is nearing dusk when the hungry children come upon the little country store tucked away on the side of the hill. dance keeps an eye out from the edge of the woods as freedom goes ahead inside. it is nearly dark before freedom returns. indian summer is drawing to its' close but there are still fireflies. finding a clearing in the woods, dance builds a small fire. the children sit down to a makeshift feast fashioned out of the stale bread and nearly rotted cheese that freedom had been given at the country store, along with some soft carrots and a few almost ripened pears dance found outside an abandoned shack while awaiting freedom's return.

having finished eating, the children are enjoying the flight of fireflies drawn to the dying fire when three soldiers appear, wearing the color of victory, arrogant from rum and in search of nonexistent spoils. the blue soldiers fall upon the two children in the convenient belief that it is their god-given right. they are like locust, ravaging indiscriminately. the children are passed around the fire well into the night until the victors, exhausted from their perversions, are well spent.

the soldiers are able to finish raping, turn over and fall fast asleep. so it is in that graceless state that the man-child sends the first to meet his maker. the soft sound of skull cracking had not awakened the other two. the soldier had not yelled but instead let out only the softest whimper. the second soldier awakens and cries out once just before dance brings the same stone down again and again, crushing the emptiness between his eyes. dance turns to see the groggy third soldier rise to his feet before a bleeding freedom, having poured the remainder of the rum over his sleeping figure, lights it. dance never forgets the perplexed look on the soldier's face as he dances along death's sacred fire or indeed the hollow look in the empty eyes of freedom as she calmly stands by and watches him burn.

freedom would not survive. the violations of a late summer's night prove too much for the six-year-old spirit-child. torn apart as she is, freedom dies before morning. that which lay hidden had not yet come to light but the sun would become insistent soon, forcing its' arrival upon the carnage held now only in darkness. instantly, as it is with dawn it was no longer night and the greatness of the gettin' up morning gone, forever misplaced.

dazed, suddenly alone, bloody and sore, dance, terrified by the loss of freedom and realizing the potential consequences to his actions doesn't even attempt to bury her. laying freedom between massive roots at the base of an ancient tree, dance covers freedom in the tiny little purpled flowers he finds there. dance tells freedom,

-goodbye,

before turning to walk away. the man-child dance walks nonstop day and night and day again until his traumatized, undernourished body will carry his tortured soul no further. the sky thunders before releasing a torrential downpour as night begins to fall again. weary, unmindful of the lightning storm, the man-child sits his depleted frame down beneath a great tree, so tired he falls flat into a puddle and sleeps where he lies in the rain. it is only by the grace of god he did not drown.

✳

seven

in the path of dance

old miss margaret finds dance's crumpled, wet body outside her flap that sunday morning. knowing if she did not take in the man-child she would have no good luck, miss margaret carries his dead weight up the one step platform into her earthen straw hut. after all she would have done the same thing for any stray found on her doorstep. besides once she gets him inside, dries him off and looks at him good, she couldn't have thrown away the dark brown angel firmly held in a fever grip from hell.

the man-child comes in and out of consciousness as, intent on consuming what little life left, the fever runs its' course. although her old wrinkled hands hold the ancestral healing skills of her mothers' and the secrets of the woods she has since discovered, miss margaret finds herself locked in a serious struggle for the man-child's continued presence this side of the grave. miss margaret has to fight, almost losing him a couple of times to the shadows. his injuries aren't all that great but his will to return weak. from the other side she feels the awful pull of a powerful little spirit but miss margaret is diligent, determined that no one who found their way to her home would die, not on her watch.

>   -no, it just plain bad luck and i ain't havin'
>   none of it.

the dark angel whimpers,

>   -freedom, freedom,

over again and again in his unconsciousness. when the fits
of rage came, the man-child thrashed about until miss margaret thought his small frame would break itself apart.
silently she held him down then wiped his face with a cool
rag before gently rocking him back to sleep.

taking off his pants to wash him, miss margaret couldn't help
but notice the bruises which covered his body, the dried
bloodstains mingled with feces she found there nor the
bloody orifice from which vileness continually oozed for
the first two days. this she cleans and bathes with herbs and
salts. in all the years to come miss margaret never spoke on
it,

>   -a man got's to be left some kinda dignity.

having lived free and as a slave, she knew how important
dignity was. dance awakens to find the blue-black face of

miss margaret studying him, the deep-set coal black eyes staring. he has no idea where he is or for how long he has slept. a course grunting sound of approval escapes from somewhere deep within her throat,

-ummmph! guess you'll live.

miss margaret gets up from her seat by his pillow, where she has spent the better part of a week nursing her stray back to health, stretching. on the cushion slowly fading, the imprints of her buttocks remain.

looking around the small hut dance sees he lies in the center of a round room near a sunken fire pit on a pallet made of straw and old rags. the woman's manner is gruff but her service kind. there is no softness as she grabs him up into a sitting position before bringing a bowl of black broth for him to eat. as he is being fed dance studies this tall blue-black women in men's clothing to whom he owes his life. dance notices she has no hair underneath the worn white bandana which she wears tied up on her head. despite the closeness of the fire he is still very cold. dance realizes there is only the one bed in the room and recognizes the generosity of spirit he has been afforded by this dark stranger.

-thank you ma'am. my name is dance.

-hmmm,

she clears her throat,

  -eweryone call me miss margaret... and you's welcome,

she whispers, well pleased by his manners. the rain falls softly upon the matted straw mud roof. inside the quiet of the
hut the man-child, revived by the warmth of the broth,
begins to remember. when freedom's face returns before
him, covered in purple flowers as he last remembered her,
dance cannot hold back his tears and begins to cry.

realizing there is no comfort for the torn man-child, miss
margaret offers none, choosing instead to mend dance's
ragged pants that have been washed.

※

eight

in the path of dance

dance remained under miss margaret's guidance from man-child into manhood. during the course of the journey dance grew to know the ways of healing and the laws of conjuring. a solitary woman of few words,

-ole marg'ret,

as she calls herself, never smiles. she has little use of conversation or people and shuns their company.

-too much ag'tation.

dance is still by nature and miss margaret sees in this a great potential. dance is so quiet she sometimes would forget he was there. dance could sit in the same spot all day watching a shaft of sunlight circumnavigate the earthen hut.

miss margaret, a conjure woman, seer, worker of roots and afrikan by birth could bring back to life almost anything she found before fully dead and she could truly kill almost anything she found alive. schooled in its' secrets, she spoke the ancient green language of her village as had her mothers and grandmothers before. if she sat very still from across a great expansive the faint smell of incense mixed with the familiar sound of shakeres slowly enveloped her senses. nzinga, as she had been called, could still make out the faces of her mothers seated around the ancient medicine hut as they had done during her womanhood training before her village had been overrun. she could not stop memory there and it continued to flow to the brown river waters which carried a virgin of near marrying age from the interior of her continent and delivered a slave girl to the ship of her captive violations.

although separated these many years from any semblance of her people by distances of unforgiving waters and the repeated cruelties of chattel-hood, still she remembered how to build a hut, her fingers how to trace roads within reeds creating a basket that could hold water and retained within the palms of her hands the healing wisdom which belonged to the house of medicine woman to which she was born, of which praise psalms have been sung for longer than anyone could remember.

miss margaret's knowledge of plants accounted for her free-dom. it was during one sunday's usual dinner fare when miss margaret warned all she would,

–not to eat,

of her often requested stuffed wild turkey with acorn stuffing that the slaves quietly slipped away, before spores amid adjacent poisons caused tongues to turn purple and swell, blocking the required access of air causing all who had ingested the family favorite to suffocate and die. while the not quite cold crumbs of the delicious stuffing still clung onto the dying lips of her hated massa with all who shared his table's fate that late summer afternoon, miss margaret simply stepped over the bodies, quietly walked off the slave farm and took to the woods. living alone by her wits for near on fifty years, she was truly a free black woman long before freedom and well after slavery. in all that time miss margaret learned to live without the comfort of human kindness, having been shown so little on her journey.

-life be hard if you gets to live it and harder still if it ain't yourn to live.

ultimately understanding the divinity within nature, miss margaret believed things happen for a reason, the brown angel had been sent to her. over time the relationship between miss margaret and dance grew. in all the years since walking off the slave farm miss margaret never noticed her loneliness and until encountering the vulnerability of the little brown boy never felt love. through out the years they spend together miss margaret never hugs or shows any outward display of affection to the boy dance as he grows to manhood, it was not her way but it is in his hoodoo education though that miss margaret gives all of her love.

early one spring morning after a wind storm dance happens

upon a sparrow's nest blown from its' perch. everything he has been taught tells him not to bring the broken bird into the house but there is something in the loneliness of the baby sparrow's solitary shaking that touches a place in dance's heart. miss margaret just grunts when he starts fixing up a nest for the bird inside. over the rest of the spring dance feeds and cares for the tiny bird at the exclusion of almost everything else.

the spring soon turns to summer, which too quickly reaches for autumn and late one afternoon dance returns to find the sparrow dead. the bird had felt the flocks' call south but the doorway and the window flaps had been closed and the southern wall served as instrument of death when the bird repeatedly flew into it attempting to join the migration.

-everythin's got a place it belong to,

was all miss margaret said but dance understood. in ways like this miss margaret poured all of her understanding into his awaiting vessel. in time dance too spoke the green language. remembering the ways he had been taught by storm-chaser long ago he knew most of the goings on in the surrounding forest and his fishing nets were never empty.

at about this time miss margaret realized dance came to the table with talents of his own, one day discovering his gift for cloud shifting. coming upon him sitting, staring into the sky, she watched for a minute and realized dance was painting images with the clouds. impressed, despite herself, miss margaret could not restrain the,

-hmmm!

which escaped with a breath from her lips.

miss margaret had to admit dance was good company. most importantly dance didn't intrude on the solitude of her,

-work, as she called it.

in slavery, a woman hesitated even to love the child pushed from between her legs, knowing that life could be snatched away at any moment and never seen again. miss margaret knew so much of the cruelties which grew in the corners of hearts, had witnessed the ravages of slavery's evil and the false promise of its' reconstruction. with the knowledge of roots she possessed miss margaret had not allowed any seed to grow which her master planted inside. no matter how many times he tried she would bear no children and so lived alone these last some odd years comforted by the certainty that nowhere in the world walked a child from her body, but here, tucked away from slavery's talons, miss margaret allowed the eyes of a brown boy found delirious in the rain to stimulate her heart chakra and dance loved miss margaret back as true as any son could.

✳

nine

in the path of dance

miss margaret sees freedom's lonely spirit first as she sweeps by the harvest moon's light. freedom appears standing in the front yard, plain as day, light from the full moon cascading softly down the back of her head and off her shoulders. understanding immediately the ethereal nature of this spirit's being, miss margaret looks upon the strange child only once before turning away for miss margaret knows the visit is not for her.

around back dance rinses the pile of fish collected from his evening's nets. he has just finished cleaning fish guts and scales sit ready for disposal in the compost heap outback. two nice fish heads are already put aside for the gold and black cat only miss margaret feeds in back of the woodshed used for curing meats. dance dumps the guts then turns, encountering the unending vacuums which suffice for freedom's eyes, reflecting moonlight. she is thirsty, having traveled such a long way searching for dance and the last vestige of kindness known in a life viciously ripped short. she drinks in the sight of dance. he searches her face for any recognizable signs of the innocence known before freedom's spirit had been released. freedom beckons dance to walk with her and gently she attempts to place her small child's hand into his but there is nothing for him to grasp onto. silently falling into a familiar cadence, the lost spirit walks beside the found soul for the better part of that early evening before she is gone.

when dance comes to bed miss margaret is silent. she never questions him because usually she already knew any answer before dance could give it and so she never asks him about the little girl spirit which had come to visit.

dance would encounter freedom only two more times, when she comes to find him on the day of fire and when she leaves on the night of manhood.

✳

ten

in the path of dance

the birds of prey are first to gather high up, circling the sky. they have the best vantage to wait for death. it is the hyenas and jackals, those ground scavengers, who follow, drawn by the putrid scent of decaying flesh and fetid fear. at dusk dance, returning from the brook with his day's catch, clearly sees the arc of flames shoot high above the trees. dropping the woven straw basket and pole, he runs towards the backwoods hut. there had been evidence of riders over the last few days. in all these years continued talk and rumor about some old black conjure woman living in the backwoods out behind the swamp land would resurface but miss margaret held so little contact with the outside world the tale became legend.

dropping down to the ground before reaching the clearing dance observes a shadow of cinders on the ground along with the corpse of a recently burnt cross, the shed it ignited smoldering still. it is from this dance had seen fire in the sky. wrapped in a white shawl, standing before the entrance way of her hut, miss margaret faces the gang of hooded riders, fearlessly, with the thumb and first two fingers of her left hand cocked strangely towards the masked terrorists, cursing them. as dance edges closer he picks up her voice on the wind,

> -these here woods, they's mine. the ground you's
> stand-in' on, i claims it, it belong to me. i'll die tonight
> sure but there's not a one of yous will ever leave these
> woods alive... these here woods, they's mine, you hear?

and with that dismissive miss margaret calmly turns, bends
her back and enters her hut, pulling down the matted flap
behind her.

the riders are confused, never before encountering a colored
woman so secure in her power. despite their miserable souls
they felt something new, fear. it is getting darker and the
waxing moon lies hidden behind clouds. the realization
becomes apparent that they could kill her but in the absence
of this colored woman's fear have no other means to control her. they don't like it nor are they willing to admit their
own terror to each other, so after a bit of grumbling and
cursing among themselves leave with the promise of a terrible return.

undetected in the dark, a silhouetted dance crosses furtively. the moon decides to peek out from in between the
clouds at the moment dance arrives at the front of the hut.
he calls miss margaret's name in a loud whisper. usually he
would have gone in with no warning but he doesn't want
to surprise her, not after what he witnessed earlier. when he
pulls back the flap miss margaret stands ready, cradling her

shotgun.

-boy it a good thing i hears your woice, 'cause i's fix'in' to blow off who-so-ever's head was sneak-in' up. shore glad them riders didn't get you.

she chuckles,

-they ain't got much use for an old 'oman like me but you just the age for them to be hateful... not that they ever needs excuse.

-they gonna come back miss margaret, you know that.

-yes i do boy, yes i do.

-don't you think we should leave?

-and go where?

she questions,

-and go where? i's too old to run.

it had been years since the brown child was left at her doorstep, abandoned by the storm. miss margaret had grown the skinny sycamore sapling into a tall young man. dance studied well and even miss margaret had to admit dance was now nearly as powerful as she. he had the gift of sight and could tell when the rains were coming or just the right time to stand in the stream to catch a basket of fish or how to pick the sweetest melon from the vine. he knew how to call the name of the wind who would then share with dance a few of the love secrets from far away places, hidden promises and whispered messages she carried on her back. dance in turn treasured the wind, understanding that the confidences she held were too numerous to count. this evening the wind held only a premonition of disaster.

miss margaret sits up all night in the doorway of the hut, her loaded shotgun and sleeping black and gold cat on her lap. dance isn't sure if she sleeps at all. there is a fierce rain shower late and afterwards the new morning promises to dawn bright. dance finally dozes off sometime after the storm before being awakened by miss margaret who sends him out to retrieve his pole and last night's catch if it hadn't already been claimed by some wildlife. the woods are thick with unfinished foreboding when dance steps outside into the predawn air. he barely reaches his basket and pole when dance hears the sound of rapidly approaching hooves. before he can react the riders rage in and without as much as exchanging a spoken word surround the little backwoods hut, douse it with kerosene and set the thatched roof on fire.

with little regard for his own well being dance leaps up and runs back attempting to reach miss margaret but two of the riders intercept and hold him. dance fights to free himself screaming for miss margaret to get out.

before long the thatched hut begins to expire. just as the frame of the little hut looks about to fall the burning cloth hanging at the entrance opens and the slow motion figure of miss margaret takes four steps toward the riders, her clothes in flames and burning cat at her side. there is an eerie silence as a fragile uncertainty holds. miss margaret never cries out and not even a sound utters from her cat. her left hand is up as it had been earlier and her mouth moves in silent prayer. dance watches miss margaret's standing figure incinerate.

it is the last thing the vigilantes see for at the moment the old woman's charred remains hit the ground the light of sight vanishes from the eye of every rider and horse. with the onset of sudden blindness the riders find themselves in confusion as beasts which serve their transport become panicked and the ensuing chaos proves ultimately to be the conveyance of their promised nightmare. on unsighted horses, ridden by riders now blind, pathways are no longer clear, thwart with branches and trees, knocking riders off horses and under the oncoming hooves of other sightless mounts. the resulting debacle the fulfillment of miss margaret's curse.

the devastation is insurmountable, the remains of miss margaret and her cat still cremating upon the ruins of what had been his home. dance stands perfectly still for most of that morning amazed and shocked amidst the havoc and mayhem which reins down. in an almost catatonic state dance turns and again with nothing but the clothes on his back walks off without direction.

dance wanders aimlessly for a long, long time, for years outside his mind, never noticing freedom's spirit quietly walking ahead to guide him.

＊

eleven

1804

in the path of a-che

the ship finally docked, another middle passage endured. the cargo poured upon night sands like pounds of shrimp. warmed by a rising sun, the scared shackled souls slowly untangle themselves seeking to reclaim their limbs and the balance of earth.

a-che stands that cloudy midday atop a wooden auction block. from her vantage point above the unintelligible babble of raging ghosts she watches a pod of gray and white dolphins swim solemnly near the shore, in the shadow of the ship. she has survived the crossing, many have not. taken, defiled many times as all the women had been, a-che proved a ghostly diversion for the long months at sea. as she listens to the drone of guttural sounds and gestations below she suddenly hears for the first time the faint patter of a racing heartbeat centered somewhere deep within herself. finally it is her time and as her breasts are handled and her privates fondled a-che silently prays that the child she carries belongs to ladji for it would mean that her line had been closed to violation.

a-che is parceled off along with the rest of the cargo and soon tied behind a mule and carriage along with three males, one warrior age, one age of manhood training and a little boy of no more than five. it is well after dark when the tired parade stops before three sad dilapidated structures scattered across a little less than an acre of rocky uneven ground and spindly knarled trees, whose foreboding branches entwine, keeping audience along its' perimeter. a-che, alongside the other slaves, is taken to a three sided wooden pen beside one of the structures, where all, without even as much as a sip of water, are secured for the night. she could feel the stares of hidden eyes peering from within the surrounding darkness but exhaustion from the relentless march wills a-che to sleep.

she is awakened at first light by the movement of two women dressed in the skins of her captors but clearly the same complexion as herself. they furtively look around before revealing fruits, bread and something she later learns is called cheese. they have kind faces but speak only the garbled mumblings of her captives. it is a good thing that the two woman brought some food for it is all they were to eat for the next two days.

soon they are on their way again and it seems to a-che that they spend all day walking uphill. the open fields giving way to tree lined paths and by night it grows quite cold. the captors build a small fire and sit beside it while the slaves are tied down and left to huddle amongst themselves for warmth. during the middle of the night it commences a slow steady drizzle and just before dawn there is a great downpour.

in the morning the uphill climb becomes steeper, filled with rocks and seemed would never end when suddenly, sometime before dusk, the land levels off. finally they confront a small patch of buildings comprising the town at the top of the mountain to which they have been brought.

※

twelve

in the path of a-che

a-che is never to hear her name called again. the next six months prove to be the most bizarre of her life. it is not an easy adjustment. she now wears the coverings and slowly begins to learn the tongue of captivity. she is given over to a white-haired woman named mable whose assigned job, besides cooking, seems to be to show her the ways of slavery. a-che's tasks are to feed, water and clean after the cow, chickens, goat and pigs, to keep neat the shack which she and mable share with them, to wash clothes and pick what fruit remains on the trees until the cold white rain began to fall. her other duty was to allow massa to climb on top and do his business whenever he wanted which turned out to be at least four or five days in seven. it seems massa had no other woman so a-che was on duty whenever he had need. it didn't stop even after her stomach grew, he then just turned her over and continued with his vileness.

by the time that the cold begins to subside a-che, now called mary, has learned a few words as she watches her belly reach fullness. she survives that winter only because she believes she carries ladji's child within. as her time grows near she begins to worry. she had been too young to enter the birthing compound and having missed womanhood training knows not what to expect. she is always tired even with the help that mable offered when she could. at the time the flowers bloom and the buds on the tree burst so does a-che.

the sun was just beginning to set and all of her chores were finished. she had just begun walking toward the barn and a well earned rest when suddenly she catches her breath and doubles over. nothing prepares her for that first pain. it is unlike anything she has ever experienced before, as if her insides were about to break out. she lets out a peculiar sound somewhere between a moan and a scream. mable comes running. she's had her eye on her all day as mary was acting that vacant kind of peculiar that always seems to pre-cede birth. she guides mary into the barn and leads her to a pile of old rags gathered for just this purpose. mable knows this will be a long night.

she is wrong. the baby seems to leap from a-che's womb. as soon as she gets her comfortable it seems the baby's here. when the head crowns a-che sends up one last prayer between contractions. in the next wave the baby turns, releases it shoulders and for the first time a-che can see her child. she doesn't yet know the sex but the almost born has the color of its' father, ladji. a-che gives a shout of praise as the baby falls into mable's waiting hands. there is no doubt what she will call the baby. she has thought of nothing else since she first felt her move. in answer to mable's question she replies in her halting english,

-nana. nana baby.

suddenly a-che begins to bleed. when mable can't stop the flow she ventures to go in and tell massa. there was no need. she finds him in the front room on the floor passed out, she could smell the rum on his breath. try as she might it was impossible to awaken him. when he does that next morning he finds mable holding the inconsolable child, sitting next to its' mother who sleeps the quiet sleep of the dead.

there is no confusion in his mind. he has no one to feed this new life and the loss of property he has to chalk up to bad luck. he will be able to sell the child and maybe she would bring in enough to buy a male goat so as not to be a total loss. he shakes his head as he slowly turns to leave, after all she had been a young piece of meat.

only the orphaned baby faintly hears the dolphins' haunting cries across the stillness found that terrible morning.

※

thirteen

1895

in the path of time

time came, set out her pile of quilts on a folding table at the crossroads and began talking to anyone who would listen. sold a few quilts too but folks mostly came for the talk. time could carry on a conversation, truth is the girl could jaw! time would start to weave a story and despite yourself there was no way for you to escape. time would obscure just enough of the through line so that you had no choice but to ask a question and once you were drawn into conversation you were done. it wasn't that time talked about herself, more often she got you to tell something and suddenly it was your business being discussed. time would talk to folks, telling truths about their lives from their most secret desires gathered from their thoughts where they fell like acorns at her feet.

no one ever seemed to mind. that was another of her qualities for although she talked all up in folks' affairs, no one ever appeared to care. time could discuss things so personal that folk did not even talk about to themselves and yet in time's mouth their private business seemed as natural-ly placed as daylight. in time folks grew to depend on the guidance and wisdom of her council. a strong red-bone, had she been born on the farm time would have brought a handsome sum. tall and substantial, time feared no one. she could beat most women or men but never had to fight. she could out talk all but the most gifted of the sisterhood, though once they met her most women-folk seemed to like her despite themselves. time didn't need an audience though. time would talk when someone was there, she would talk to no one. one might think time needed to keep talking in order to continue breathing. time just plain talked, it didn't matter to wind, to clouds, to trees but most often to power.

as a child time promised herself to power. she met him once in a grove when she was a child. they played together for the better part of an afternoon. she had been fascinated by the luminescence of his skin. he had been such fun. it was just that one day and she had seen him no more. he promised to return. it was why she waited at the crossroads for if he passed this way again she surely would not miss him.

time's rarely alone. at ease in the company of men-folk, time is never seen with any one man. she knows them for what they are and understands them. the common belief among most women-folk was that it would take precious little convincing to get time down on one of her quilts. time knew what folks thought and she did not care.

-folks believes what they wants to for as long
as it suits them.

time laughed simply,

-they ain' interested in truth. folks can give away they
power if they wants to... i chooses to pay them no never
mind.

men-folk in their turn never seemed to assume with time
and in that way gave her their respect. the truth is time was
still a virgin when dance happened along that sultry summer
night. time was sitting out with her quilts under the heavy
solstice moon,

-conversatin' with the wind,

when a tight sinewy frame on this dark brown-skinned full-
lipped man with eyes of fire crosss her path. time attempts
to engage him in conversation but dance proves elusive. a
man of few words, he truly had little to say, having just
recently returned to his mind.

dance found himself wandering alongside a riverbank, his
face wet as if he'd been crying or had it been rain, he was-
n't sure. dance has no idea how long he had been gone or
indeed from where he returned but his river reflection
showed gray at the edges of his beard. his last conscious
memory turning to leave miss margaret's pyre. having

retreated so far into his grief, for years he could not find the pathway's return or retrace his steps. he must have come full circle though for when dance returned to his mind he did not remember having traveled this way before.

dance had not spoken with anyone for so many years he had all but forgotten speech, making conversation with this dark dance of silence prove to be time's greatest challenge. even at his most loquacious, dance was never a conversationalist. having grown up in the stillness of miss margaret's company there had been little need, words only used for mundane chores. any real communication between miss margaret and dance had been unnecessary as she knew most everything through their hoodoo or earth connection as miss margaret preferred to call it. anyway, dance's study had been listening not speaking, proving it nearly impossible for time to gather dance into her talking web. dance truly had nothing to say. for the first occasion in life she had to work at making conversation. time's natural banter fell short and her well tuned skills failed. time was undaunted. she called upon all she had learned in her stretch at the crossroads. reaching deep into dance's being time grabbed the edge of the slightest thread unraveling enough to eventually pull dance into revealing his story. time is nearly blinded by the truths that fall that night. time is drawn to the strength of solitude and the depth of sorrow she discerns in dance's eyes.

dance looks at this quilt woman of the crossroads. he sees a quiet beauty in her face, a grace in the movement of her hands and a voice he could listen to... he is attracted to her but there is an insatiable look in her eyes, a hunger that frightens him. the wisdom of miss margaret should have had dance moving away from time without delay. he even begins focusing on the wind on which he depended for his next direction to take. dance is looking off into the horizon when time offers softly,

-ain't no need in continuin' to look for freedom...
it ain't a fo' real place. it's the place you's standin' in.
freedom a place in you.

there is a long pause before,

-won't you please stay long enough for i to make
you a quilt?...

that was all. that was the proposal.

dance is silent as he looks up at the stars and around at the blue mountains that nestle this little village. he suddenly feels very tired. then he looks into the moon lit eyes of time and dance, who'd known so little softness, allows himself to fall beneath the spell of this quilt women at the crossroads and for a while the time they spend together seems to fly.

✳

fourteen

in the paths of time

time is sitting quilting on the porch, so intensely focused she doesn't notice dance's arrival. dance had that quality where he could move without anyone noticing or sometimes he could stand so still you would forget he was there at all. time had no idea how long dance had been standing watching her work. quilting was a meditation in which she never noticed the passage of time. she quilts almost in a trance like someone possessed. sitting down to quilt was usually the last thing time remembered until putting down her needle and reemerging. it is only then that time would see her work as if for the first time.

time had been working on dance's quilt for nearly a year and it was almost finished. since meeting dance time sat at the crossroads and thought of power less, working on dance's quilt demanding so much of her time. it had taken the better part of a season to allow the pattern to find itself in her mind before it began to manifest itself into a quilt. now time couldn't seem to put the quilt down for long before it called her back again. putting down her needle, time looks up and into the eyes of dance. there is something so sad and gentle in these eyes set in silence that whatever secrets they hold time fears may be too sacred for her to ever fully share. time knows at this moment just how deeply she wants dance yet he's only promised to stay until the quilt's finished. now that it is nearly done time's a little scared for she understands she will never love this way again.

dance gently takes the quilt off of her lap and lays it across the banister that wraps around the farmhouse. standing in the yard, a little ways back from the porch, dance could see the quilt's overall circular pattern of gold and red mountains ranges with two golden moons dotted against an indigo sky. dance looks happy as he stands admiring time's handiwork and time is well pleased. the rest of the afternoon they spend quietly watching colors change in the sky. dance shows off with some cloud hunting in which time is more than a little intrigued. again and again dance chooses a little cloud and concentrates on sending warm air to its' center. slowly within a few minutes just that one cloud would fade away. dance shows time and she is also able to but stops after confessing she feels troubled that she might be hunting some cloud's child. dance also stops, touched by her compassion.

time looks again at this dance man. he is surely,

-the waters,

of which the elders speak when referring to,

-still waters runnin' deep.

watching the setting sun, time and dance eat left over fried chicken, corn bread and potato salad on the porch. it starts out as a wager when time challenges dance to an arm-wrestle, after all she could beat all of the women in town and most of its' men. it turns into a wrestling match then tickling contest and when time's face goes into the potato salad bowl finally into a full fledged food fight. when they finish and look at themselves covered in chicken bones, potato salad and crumbs, they laugh and laugh again and again. time finds herself holding onto dance at dusk. she never lets go and dance never gets up to leave. that night, dance and time take each other on the unfinished quilt.

the moon slowly rises, watching the lovers as they lay. from across the clearing, shaking her head, freedom also watches. it will be for the last time. dance looks up just in time to see freedom's spirit slowly turn and walk away.

✳

fifteen

in the path of time

power arrives with the storm. biliously bleached white sheets blow on the line in the yard. wind gusts again and again before time becomes aware of her sheets. for some reason in the midday light of this midsummer afternoon the bleached sheets seem particularly bright. everything in the day has a newness to it, time had lain with dance last night and for dance time stopped. the morning dawns with such promise that had time or dance the wisdom of age they would have been more wary of the stillness and its' pregnant silence. the quality of light changes quickly, all at once. dark clouds ride in like night riders blighting light from day. as brightness changes shadows grow and pathways open. it was just a flash storm that came suddenly upon them and would pass as quickly away.

behind the house dance is drawing water from the well. he barely has time to bring up the near full bucket before being pelted by thick hot drops. dance just finishes replacing the irregularly shaped slab of wood to cover the well when he hears a tremendously loud clap of thunder. turning the corner of the porch dance witnesses the jagged lightning rod's descent from the sky. following its' intended path to conclusion, dance could do nothing as time drops down surrounded by swirling clouds of sheets, dust and fire. time barely has a moment to reach her sheets before brilliance flashes, hitting precisely between her eyes, *blinding and sending time tumbling backwards towards ground and far beyond to a stark beach of hot white sand surrounding a tiny lake of crystal clear blue water. seeming almost to cease breathing the entire enclosure, encircled by an adolescent grove of white birch, holds onto its' secrets tightly, giving none away.*

in the center of the oasis, high on a mound of white sand, sits power. it is he who summons, knowing since her first call that time has been stalking him. reticent to act power but watched time set her wares at the crossroad. power, so busy watching as time turned to dance allowed time to be taken. now, as power approaches, naked, totally devoid of color, in possession of one massive erection and set on indefinable destruction, time is paralyzed, powerless to do anything to stop him. without making one sound and with absolutely no regard to time's voiceless screams, power ravaged time over and over again unmercifully, as only a jealous lover could, until totally spent, fully satiated and completely secure in the certainty of his wrathful success, power is as suddenly gone...

time lay surrounded by bleached white sheets, now soiled. by the time dance reached her he had seen enough to conclude that time was probably dead. it is a thought dance would not allow his mind to hold onto and instead chooses not to think as he runs to the singed sheets blowing around the unmoving figure stricken in the middle of the yard. when dance reaches time she lay there, eyes rolled back, shaking and for what seems like an eternity time convulses. dance finds a stick to put between her teeth to keep her from biting her tongue. there is smoke coming from between her eyes where lightning burned into her head. they are isolated and there is no one within yelling distance. dance was torn between going for help or staying but couldn't leave time out there alone. sitting on the burnt ground, placing time between his gangly legs, dance centers himself and calms his breathing. working mostly from instinct, dance follows the way miss margaret taught him, first allowing his hands to float above time's body feeling for the life pulse within and once located dance gives into inner law, concentrating only on reaching earth's rhythm below. bringing it up through his body much like a plant intakes water he connects that link to time and then dance concentrates on nothing.

when time finally returns she finds the concerned eyes of dance staring intently. looking around at her recently bleached sheets strewn across the yard, time has no idea for how long she has lain there. the storm had passed and the cloudless sky nearly blue again. time remembers little and nothing after the lightning hit until the look in dance's eyes but she is sore. dance makes her lie still for a while and then carries time as far as the rocking chair on the front porch. time watches as dance, still in disbelief of the strange miracle of resurrection witnessed, unceremoniously collects the soiled sheets. dance could not help thinking over and over again,

-she should be dead! time should be dead!

time still tingles and a strange halo hugs everything in her field of vision. it is as though there is a soft distance between time and the space around her.

as dance returns with the sheets he notices the scar that time would carry to her grave. dance drops the sheets in a porch corner and comes over to look at time's forehead more closely. power had marked time in the shape of lightning zig-zagging between the corner of the left eye before it vee shapes down across nose to the corner of the right nostril. the singed skin is somewhat iridescent and at the right angle almost seems to glow. time had not noticed the scar until dance brings it to her attention. once done she thinks of little else. lightly touching her face and running her finger, time could feel the slightly raised skin under her hand. time begins to release a quiet stream of tears. constantly amazing are the things taken for granted without appreciation. time had never paid much attention to her looks, people having always spoken of her as,

-a pretty red-bone,

and time accepted her looks without much fanfare as a given. suddenly devastating was the thought of permanent disfigurement as time immediately understood the missive of missing water while staring at a dry well, appreciation for her life having been spared already fading in importance. inconsolable, time rocks on the porch until well after sunset. dance sits on the steps in front of her as he too witnesses the sun's glorious descent. the sky had been washed after the afternoon thunderstorm and the sunset colors fresh, vibrant. beneath the changing canopy dance reflects on his day as he did every evening, something else which dance attributed to miss margaret. looking over at time dance realizes how close he had come to losing her. dance refused to accept losing anyone else he loved.

time, wrapped in dance's unfinished quilt and dance, in silence within the shadows of approaching night, fall deeply in love and before laying down dance proposes marriage to which time accepts.

✳

sixteen

in the path of time

        -marked,

is what folks would say,

    -by the hand of god, by the very hand of god,

when the story of the quilt woman of the crossroads' dance
with lightning had been told and retold again. folks began
to visit. sister-women would bring by a covered pie plate
to the steps of the porch,

  -heard you was doing poorly, just brought a little some-
           thin' for you after your accident,

hoping for an invitation, which never came, to sit a spell.
else they arrived in small groups,

    -to take a look-see at some of your new quilts.

time knew it was to look at her scar and see for themselves
if all that they had heard was true, a tale so outrageous there
was little need for embellishment. after nearly losing her to
the power within the storm dance refused to waste any

64

time. he spoke to the minister the next morning and they were to be married the following sunday after service. it was to be a simple affair.

it rains and rains all that august morning, heavily. time's maid of honor, bernice, spent the week on time's gown, fitting and adjusting hem lines and sleeve lengths and sewing buttons and stitching until everything was just perfect. satisfied, bernice stands back and allows time to see her reflection. as she admires her creation bernice whispers,

-girl, you look so beautiful,

time looks into the mirror and is again startled by the fresh scar she is sure she will never get used to. it was still all she could see. tears begin to well up in her soft brown eyes. the horror of disfigurement continuing to grow daily as does her resentment. time had not yet recognized the lightning strike as invocation and invitation to her reign of power. never more in the last week than at this moment, time questions again,

-why? why me?

bernice, time's oldest and dearest friend, sees the look in time's eye and quietly places the lace veil. it covers the scar and time looks precious in the one family treasure that her grandmother had passed on. the lace veil had a story of its' own to tell. it seems some old white woman who first

65

owned nana baby, time's grandmother, had taught her how to make lace. the old lady was a task master and nana baby hated her and her hateful thread but never-the-less became a great maker of lace. when the old lady got sick and died nana baby, now a fully grown woman, was sold with the estate and given to another massa's daughter as a birthday present. the two women were nearly the same age and despite their disparate stations in life appreciated each other's company, nana baby providing the audience needed for her mistress' entertainment and waiting in the house seemed preferable to the toil of the fields.

when time came for her mistress to marry, nana baby was instructed to sew a wedding veil. only the finest imported silk thread was to be used and she given three months to complete her task. nana baby works tirelessly on this veil, which was to be floor length and to have this very intricate rose on the vine pattern interwoven within. when she finishes everyone agrees it is the finest craftsmanship they had ever witnessed. her mistress was ecstatic and since there was so much extra decides to make nana baby a gift of a small piece of discarded lace. nana baby and the wagon boy were,

-fixin' to jump the broom.

massa had given permission for their wedding to take place the day after his daughter's during the fourth of july celebration, the one day slaves have off besides christmas morning. as the time of the weddings draws near excitement grows within the household until about a week before when preparations suddenly come to a halt and all hell breaks lose. seems the intended buys, beds and then runs off with a slave girl from one of the neighboring farms. he had not just lain with her, the type of social behavior deemed acceptable but much to the embarrassment of nana baby's mistress and the chagrin of her father and their entire church-going community, there is talk he tried to get them married. of course there wasn't any preacher in the county who would perform such an unholy act but this outrage was deemed totally unacceptable. nana baby learns of all this through whisperings at back doors and in conversations overheard when white-folks took such little notice of a colored presence they talked to each other in front of you as they would any of the farm animals they own.

there was such a shouting, crying and a breaking of china the likes of which nana baby had never seen as her mistress adjusted to the shame of the situation. it was a bad time for all the slaves, especially nana baby on whom the jilted bride took out her anger, blaming nana baby for being a female slave but mostly because with her own nuptials approaching, nana baby was happy. on the day of the aborted wedding nana baby is instructed to take all of the wedding clothes out behind the fields and burn them. her mistress naturally includes the small piece given to nana baby who could not bring herself to burn her lace veil that she had spent so much time and love on. so nana baby hid the veil by burying it in the woods behind the fields and when her mistress asked her for it nana baby refused to give it to her. now slaves had very little that they could call their own and privacy not included among them. when the search of quarters does not yield the veil her mistress orders her whipped but still nana baby does not tell. her mistress then has nana baby's wedding stopped and plans made to sell the wagon boy south at the next auction. on the morning nana baby and the wagon boy run for their freedom she goes back and digs up the veil and it has been in the family every since, comprising the something old for time's wedding.

the thunderstorm stops for just the half hour it takes time to travel from her front porch up the hill to the little wooden church before starting up again just as she begins her march down the two rows of pews, which suffice for an aisle. the ground is soaked and the hem of time's gown tinged forever with the red of the clay roads. the little church is half filled. the bride's family sits to the left of the makeshift altar and as dance has no family the other members of the congregation take it upon themselves to fill in to the right. since both her parents are dead time is walked down the aisle by her two aunts, her mother's sisters. both aunts have been protective of time since her mother's death. there had been a second child at the time of time's birth, a little boy who stuck and refused to be born. her mother had only an instant to name time before she was gone. they buried mother and son together and the two aunts raised time from birth.

dance had never seen anything more beautiful than his bride dressed in white, flanked by her two aunts. dance understood little of beauty and the mysteries of women. dance had known precious few women in his life, only miss margaret and she had held no interest in beauty. dance bought a brand new broom. lightning flashes and thunder chants in the background as vows are exchanged before time and dance jump. time's light skinned and older aunt affection cries during the ceremony while the younger and darker aunt cinnamon just grunts. she is not overly impressed with this dance. she had barely been introduced properly. she just doesn't understand the hurry and so she is suspicious about this rush to the altar.

time does not want the veil lifted but there is no other way for dance to kiss his bride so she acquiesces. the reception afterwards is also a small and quiet event until just after they cut the cake. it is then that the face of power reappears before time's eyes. time recognizes him and instantly begins to sob uncontrollably. the elders brush it off as release of nerves, dance isn't so sure. there was nothing that time could tell him or anyone. time can't stop crying and the severity of her tears surprise even herself. dance gently holds time in his arms as slowly people make excuses and begin to go home in the storm which ceaselessly continues to rage.

the next morning time awakens early and arises without waking dance. she quietly steps out on the porch to sit among the comforting songs of early morning birds. as she rocks on the porch with dance's unfinished quilt on her lap, time tries to make sense of this last week. it has been such a whirlwind starting with the lightning strike. well actually she could begin with making love for the first time the night before and then the flash which she still sees if she closes her eyes. she tries to remember what happened next. she could see his eyes. that is how she recognized him when she recalled his face at the church. time knows now she had seen power during that time when she blacked out but that is all she allows herself to remember.

time and dance have already been married three weeks when she misses her flow. in the period to come she would wonder if it was the lightning strike which split her egg in two.

❋

seventeen

in the path of time

deciding on the need for gold near the corners, time returns to her rocking chair on the porch and puts the quilt back on her lap. she is adding the final touches to dance's quilt. she could feel someone approaching. time notices her senses have heightened since the lightning strike. there is still a rumble in her ears that will not go away. it wasn't that she suddenly could hear better or see greater distances but she now noticed little details, a change of wind direction or the formation of a cloud. recently she began to hear people's thoughts and if someone stood close enough to her she could actually hear blood rushing through veins and their heart beating. by the quality of rhythms she senses, time knows it is two people approaching and as they get closer time recognizes them as her two aunts long before the bend in the road where she could see the white haired sisters slowly making their way up the path. time knows the elders are coming to look at her belly.

she this morning, for the first time, felt it move. time kept her pregnancy a secret from everyone including dance. she knew soon the time would come for him and everyone else to know but she wanted this time to herself before it became everyone else's business. today at church when the

baby moved she felt the eyes of aunt affection looking at her
with a strange smile. it must have been the way she unconsciously cradled her arms around her stomach that caused
the one aunt to force the other to walk out to time's place
that afternoon.

–how do baby girl?

–baby girl?

–how do aunt affection, aunt cinnamon?

they have always called her baby girl, never had no truck
with that time business. time is what her mother named her
though neither aunt could believe it. they had decided on
nana themselves even before their sister died.

–and what kind of name is time, anyway?

–it ain't a name, it's a thing.

–how can you look at a sweet little baby and call it time?
just don't make no sense,

but their sister had been insistent,

–it's gonna be a girl and i's gonna name this here baby
time.

just plain obstinacy thought her sisters.

-dear jesus, well, i for one ain't callin' her no such a thing,
gonna call her nana, after our sweet mother,
god rest her soul.

strange thing was time never responded to nana, not even as
a child. of course she never disrespected her aunts but she
didn't resonate to the name. she was time, that's the only
name her mother had given her and all she had left of her
and time held onto it fiercely. today though her aunts have
come on a mission of greater importance than names and
aunt affection wastes no time getting right down to the
point,

-girl, you with child!

she declares, not even asking a question.

-and when was you gonna let a body know?

-obviously waren't no need,

smiles time, shaking her head and looking at her aunt with
little surprise. aunt affection always seemed to know certain
things, especially women things. she was the one to notice
when time had first begun to flow. it had been at least a year
later before aunt cinnamon knew anything about it.

-then it's true? how far gone are you?

asks aunt cinnamon, who begins to count weeks in her head.

-what does dance think, must be fit to burst?

-he don't know yet.

aunt affection turns up one eyebrow,

-well when you fixin' to tell him, baby girl?

-he gonna know soon enough,

chimes in aunt cinnamon with a little chuckle as she thinks of their baby girl big as a house.

-plans on tellin' him tonight.

it is then that aunt affection and aunt cinnamon smell the marble pound cake cooling on the window sill. if they had-n't been so caught up in their own excitement they would have noticed how nicely time has herself fixed up. she is wearing a new dress she's made. the white and blue looks real good against her skin and time already had that expec-tant mother's glow. aunt affection looks into the dining room and sees how nicely the table is set, a beautiful bowl of wild flowers at its' center.

-well, think it's time we was on our way home sista.

-but sista, we just got here,

answers aunt cinnamon.

-ain't even been offered a glass of lemonade or anythin',

as she rolls her eyes in the direction of her niece. before time can answer aunt affection jumps up and is starting down the three steps,

-and you ain't need to have none now. some sassafras tea coolin' at home and besides baby girl got family business to attend to. don't need us underfoot,

and with that she steps off the porch and begins bristly walking back down the hill.

-well i knows you don't expects me to run,

grumbles aunt cinnamon as she reluctantly follows,

-and ain't we's family?

time laughs as she watches the receding figures out of sight. of one thing she is sure and that is their love. just beyond the bend in the road they pass dance on his way home.

-how do miss affection, miss cinnamon. nice day.

-how do yourself dance.

returns aunt affection, smiling broadly as she gently touches his face. aunt cinnamon nods her head and chuckles,

-yes sir, a real nice day.

this show of affection from aunt cinnamon is something new for dance and he studies the faces of the two woman for a moment. as he approached the house he could see time putting away her needle. she had completed work on his quilt.

time hears dance coming long before she sees him. she learned to recognize his presence first. in the almost four months since that storming afternoon of their marriage, time could hear dance's thoughts more and more clearly with each passing day. at first it was only when they were making love. embarrassed by what she hears, she thinks it's only in her own head, then there had come his dreams. it started one night when she awakened to use the slop jar in the corner of the room. as she squatted she became aware of dances' breathing, heavy and labored. then he jerked as this dream began to take over his being. suddenly he began to kick and fight in his sleep and just as quickly time was bombarded with images of night riders circling a burning structure and on the porch an old woman and cat in flames. dance screams, waking himself and just as quickly the image fades from time's mind's eye. dance never speaks about his nightmares and time does not tell him of her discovery. the truth was time is a little nervous about her new acquisition and so she keeps her secret to herself.

now as she feels dance coming along the path she picks up images of the rock quarry where dance found work. this second sight is becoming more pronounced. she feels a flush as she catches an image of herself on the bed undressed in early morning light, after all they are still newlyweds. this gift catches time unawares again and again because images just come to her, it isn't as if she is trying to probe. although intrigued and momentarily satisfied, time realizes she might not always want to know dance's every thought. time spreads dance's finished quilt across the banister as he comes up on the porch, truly her best work. as is his custom dance takes time in his arms and kisses her before saying a word. it is one of the things about him time loves the most. dance then stands back to admire his quilt. it is truly a work of beauty. dance picks the quilt and time up and carries them both to bed and as they had done those almost four months before make sweet love on dance's quilt.

it is afterwards, before they have their late night supper, that time tells dance of their upcoming blessing and then they eat a very giddy repast. dance sits up late into the night trying to picture himself as a father. he had never known his own, not many slaves had. bought as a baby from his mama's arms, all he remembers is growing up as one of,

-hey, you chil'ren come on up here and et.

dance recalls the day he realizes that meant him. they set out the food like slop for cats out of two or three large flat bowls. children ran from wherever they were on the farm as first to food was first to feast. the image is as fleeting as it is frightening and dance removes himself from his memory and returns himself to the joy within the knowledge that time now carries his child. he promises himself it would never know hunger. he thinks of miss margaret and how happy she would have been and then he thought of freedom, of course.

dance lays down and pulls time in close to him. time is dreaming and kicking as are the babies inside. power has come to visit in her dream to see for himself the baby that had begun to move. power can sometimes be blind. that is truth for he only sees the one baby, not the two and the one baby he saw was fathered by dance.

✳

eighteen

in the path of time

dance's dreams come more frequently and as time goes on she finds her dream-catcher circle seems to grow. when the night gets still time is able to pick dreams right out of the air. at first it is only dance's dreams. they are almost always the same, the riders, the burning house, the woman and cat on fire. there is a little girl whom time would sometimes see but for the most part dance sleeps dreamless and undisturbed. of course there would be those early morning dreams time is pleased to know are always about her. after all, dance has known no other woman.

one night the babies awaken time and it is then that she knows there are two. there are stretches when they simply would not allow her sleep. sometimes she felt as if they must be fighting each other, kicking something awful. she wanted to know why it was always at night. if she walked around they would usually settle down and time finds herself in the front yard before fully awake. there are a multitude of stars out. standing there time suddenly becomes aware of a rush of images and thought forms from any number of people. time could clearly hear dance's thoughts as well as his snores but above that, though softer and more distant, time could make out a jungle of dreams.

time is intrigued and begins to experiment with the time of day she came out on her porch to listen. soon it becomes apparent to time if she sat on her porch at just the right time of night she might catch a dream or thought from anyone within the county, usually just at dawn when it's so quiet the crickets sleep and before the deep night stillness awakens the libido of the mountain village. sitting there listening, time is amazed at the details she discovers;

-missy mays pregnant again with her ninth child,

-the minister's wife fixin' to leave him with those two miserable children,

-deacon cecil's son and his goin's on up north or

-quiet girl's unrequited love for ba'y joe.

it was like having a good gossip without ever having to talk with anyone else and just about as reliable because as time begins to recognize the voices connected to the dream fragments that go floating by, she still has to ascertain if what she hears is indeed part of a dream, having its' own sense of truth or a conscious thought that might easily prove quite inaccurate because people so often lie, even to themselves, especially when asleep.

through this patchwork method of wind listening time is able to learn all types of secrets as folks are no more and quite often much less than the sum of their secrets. time could not resist the inherent power she felt in knowing private thoughts and hidden lies. it is then that time decides to return to the crossroads. after all at the crossroads she would have greater access to the lives of the people around her.

about this dance is not pleased. he is working steadily at the quarry and doesn't understand the necessity of having his pregnant wife sitting all the way out at the crossroads alone. it is true dance has seen few pregnancies, most from the distance of childhood but time, only in her second trimester is already huge. dance who of course knows nothing of the stages of pregnancy knows time is too big to be dragging herself all across the county.

-why can't you make quilts at home? what so god-all important at the crossroads?

dance, unable to deny his new bride anything, in the end succumbs. people begin to come by the crossroads again when they hear of time's return. there are those who have simply missed the good conversation time draws out from them, those who come to see the lightning scar as folks have grown to call the vee shaped keyloid which darkened over time's light skin and then of course there are the gossips. though at first few people notice, there is a difference, this time does less talking now. sometimes silent and infinitely more interested in listening, time allows for all of them to come, drawing them in turn into conversation and as they talk she listens, before they arrive and after they depart she listens and this is how she learns.

dance is not aware of the talk beginning to go around as people get a good look at time, the size she is and begin to count on their fingers. though they are careful not to breathe a word of this around aunt affection or aunt cinnamon, one of the hardest things to stop is a malicious rumor. people like to talk in everybody's business and so now the talk was of time's rush down the aisle.

-don't nobody plan a weddin' in a week...

-less'n they has to!

-runnin' to the altar so fast, a wonder she
didn't trip and fall...

and then they would laugh dry dirty little laughs. it is time who first catches a glimpse of the talk going around and at her first chance corners fannie elizabeth, the main one doing most of the talking.

-miss fannie, although it barely took me a whole week
to plan my weddin',

purposely using fannie elizabeth's own words,

-i's so glad i's only had the joy of sleepin' with just the one
man before, durin' or after the takin' of my vows...

time pauses for effect,

> -do give my best to your husband bob... and to
> his brother roy.

it was such a peculiar thing to say. time did not even look up from her quilt cuttings as she went on about the weather and the new rain coming their way but fannie elizabeth did not lose the significance of time using both brothers' names. fannie elizabeth had been carrying on an affair with her brother-in-law that both believed no one else knew anything about, until now. truth is fannie elizabeth's second son looked just like his uncle roy, though they named him earl. time never mentions roy again nor did fannie elizabeth ever again discuss time's pregnancy with anyone. after that fannie elizabeth stayed her distance from time and kept time's business well out of her mouth.

knowledge is power. the potential found in that equation proved to be more than time could stand and easily seduced by her talents, time never once gave thanks for her gifts. she had her own agenda and given the opportunity could not help herself from moving on it. time had stalked this power of her dreams, again affirming that one has to be careful what one asks for, for power was given to time or was it the other way around? was it not time who had been sacrificed in the end? it was subtle at first, a quiet distain that silently grew. time became arrogant and heady, smug in the way one can only be when one is sure one knows the answer or worse when one knows the question before it is even asked. soon time makes less and less effort to hide her gift. she stops pretending to even try to have conversation. there is no reason for she gathers all she needs from folks' passing thoughts. she would harvest information quietly at the start but as time went on she became just plain rude, jumping all into folks' business without being asked. sometimes before they even finished their thought time answered their question, dismissed their comment or contradicted their statement. slowly folks begin to notice and finally it is bernice who says something.

-time, what's goin' on here?

time looks up from the pieces she is pinning onto the batting of the new quilt and into the eyes of her oldest friend. they have known each other practically all of their lives. mama bates, bernice's grandmother had been almost like her own and on bernice's porch time learned from mama bates to quilt. time knows it is a rare and precious thing to have a grandmother, slavery allowing for so very few. time thought how truly lucky bernice was to know and have both mother and grandmother. time had aunt affection and aunt cinnamon and together they almost made up for a mother or so time thought but a grandmother, now that was something else entirely. time remembered her smell and her smile. mama bates had no teeth but her dark gums sparkled in the daylight. mama bates was quiet until she laughed; her laugh loud, raucous and contagious. mama bates would get,

-the devil,

in her eye. if time looked into the brown eyes of bernice she could see the quiet and the laughter of mama bates staring back. both comforting and disturbing, bernice had a way of looking at you which made time want to hide. she was the only one who could make time feel that way, well that is besides aunt cinnamon.

-what you mean, bernice? what you talkin' 'bout?

-don't you 'what you mean bernice' me. you know 'zactly to what i's referrin'. folks talkin' all behind your back and it ain't right.

-what ain't right? what folks sayin'?

-sayin' you all in they thoughts, like you can read they mind. folks say fannie elizabeth won't even speak your name. say you put her in the fear of god. been in church every sunday these last two months.

time laughs out loud but silently she is amazed at how accurate the grapevine is.

-and what you say, bernice?

85

-say don't know a thing but that you is
seven months pregnant. to tell you the truth you
has been actin' mighty peculiar here lately. you so
moody, can't hardly nobody talk with you.

bernice laughs,

-but then you always been ornery. seem preoccupied or
somethin' 'most all of the time tho', more than usual.
know you worried about the baby...

-babies.

-babies? what you talkin' 'bout girl?

-know there's two, just like ...

time doesn't finish the sentence but she could not help
completing the thought. time couldn't remember if bernice
knew about her brother. she must. time remembered
playing with bernice at her mother and brother's grave
behind the little white picket fence in a small enclosed
wood that would one day become the family graveyard.
time knows she will have to spend a day and go visit their
grave before the babies are born.

bernice never gets back to her original line of questioning,
so thrown is she by time's disclosure. of course bernice
knows the story of time's birth and she instinctively under-

stands time's apprehension. it now makes sense, this massive weight gain. she attributes time's moodiness to the carrying of twins as well. this same observation does not escape the attention of aunt affection. she doesn't say much but time notices that lately her aunt spends more and more time around the house and has begun to knit a second baby blanket. time refuses to stay at home. the truth is she has become dependent on listening to other people's lives. in comparison she finds the silent isolation when confined to the home front deafening.

there is a light dusting of frost on the ground the morning time decides to visit the little family cemetery. she follows the seldom taken path down pass the edge of the tree line and into the little meadow which serves as her mother's burial ground. there is still only the one grave. there should have been two but they never did find time's father. he went out hunting one day when time was five-months-old and never returned. although it was generally thought he had been found by riders and lynched somewhere, no one knew for sure.

time pays her respects. she cleans weeds from around the grave, then places flowers and fruit in a wooden bowl she had brought there for that purpose. time spends the better part of the morning at the grave and it is only as she begins to leave that she hears the voices. they are different from the voices she's heard many times in the air. these aren't in the air. time realizes they are within her belly. she listens carefully. there are no words, only a kind of humming of a tune but she recognizes them, two souls singing in harmony. time sits back and listens. it is a beautiful sound, this drone of the not yet born. it begins to lull time to sleep. time realized she could not remember ever being quite this tired before. she's been pushing hard here lately and there is still so much to get done in the next few weeks. still a matter of a crib and their corner of the room hasn't been set up yet. there is still a while or so she thinks. time begins to drift off and just before she leaves this consciousness could swear she hears a third voice join in the drone. this third voice seems to come from somewhere else outside of her body. time has just had the thought that the last voice might be coming from the grave when she falls into a deep sleep. time sleeps a sleep only expectant mothers are allowed for soon they will never sleep like this again. time sleeps so soundly she does not feel the fast moving storm's approach nor the one in her belly.

stealthily the temperature falls. the drops of freezing rain awaken time just before the first pain catches her unawares, taking away all of her breath. time has only time to look down before she feels her membrane burst and her water begin to gush. before she could scream or the steam rise from the contact of her birthing fluids on the cold ground, time found herself in hard labor.

✳

nineteen

in the path of time

aunt affection stands on the porch looking in the direction of the small graveyard. she had come over to visit with time and found her missing. she hadn't passed her niece on the country road and as big as time is aunt affection knows her niece couldn't have gone far.

-now where baby girl done got to?

aunt affection mumbles to herself. it is then she notices the fresh footprints in the soft clay road. something just doesn't feel right, especially after the rain starts and time had not returned. suddenly something takes hold of aunt affection and she grabs her shawl, throws it over her head and begins down the little used path towards the brook and the field where her sister and nephew are buried.

-baby girl where you at?

aunt affection calls as she hurries into the little meadow. the skies suddenly open up and a torrential rain begins to pour before she catches sight of time lying next to her mother's grave.

-oh my god!

was all aunt affection could manage to scream as ancient legs begin to run. aunt affection reaches her and although too early, her knowledge tells her time is definitely delivering. aunt affection has only time to push up time's dress and pull down her drawers before she has to catch and ease the little head out as the small dark brown baby boy is born. barely five pounds aunt affection's old and experienced hands could tell, she clears his airway and he lets out a scream could be heard halfway across the county. aunt affection barely has time to cover him with her shawl and lay him on his mother's chest so she could deliver the placenta when immediately afterwards contractions begin again. aunt affection raises her eyebrows and eight minutes later holds an extremely tiny girl. less than four pounds aunt affection judges and totally devoid of color,

-this second baby,

she thinks to herself,

-might not make it.

although the baby breathes spontaneously after she rips the silver caul from her face, she does not utter a sound. time puts out her arms for her second child and holds both children on her chest side by side. aunt affection softly massages and massages but time will not deliver the second placenta.

suddenly time's legs begin to shake uncontrollably. aunt affection grabs the babies just before time drops them. she worries how she is going to get time back up to the house? she knows these babies can't be out in the cold too much longer and yet aunt affection doesn't want to move time until birth has completed. suddenly the shaking stops and time delivers the second placenta, perfect in every way but totally silver in color. aunt affection goes to work cutting and tying cords, cleaning up both children and mother. aunt affection had delivered babies,

-for nigh on thirty year,

she would later tell her sister,

-ain't never seen anythin' like it in my life. the caul
and the afterbirth all silver and the baby totally white.
um um umm!.

dance, who rarely came home for lunch, is met by a crazed aunt affection gesturing wildly and calling to him, carrying a bundle up the path. aunt affection decided on taking the babies inside and then returning to get time. aunt affection knows god had answered her prayer when she turns the corner and sees dance there. he comes running.

-where's time?

is all he manages to get out before aunt affection screams,

-in there!

as she indicates the clearing behind her.

-they're both fine,

aunt affection adds as dance quizzically looks down at the bundle in her arms. dance runs towards time and gently folding his wife into his arms, he carries her home. dance is dispatched to go and bring back aunt cinnamon. the next task is setting up a place for time and her offspring to lie. so it is only later that dance goes in to look at his child, after being assured time is all right for although it was an early labor it had also been a quick and relatively painless birth. it is only as dance approaches the blanket that he realizes there are two babies, one brown and one white, both holding on to each other as they must have done in the womb. dance realized when aunt affection had said,

-they're both fine,

he assumed she meant mother and child not brother and sister. the baby boy cries and time's milk comes in just fine. she feeds them both at once and they both eat ravenously. once satiated they fall asleep, clinging to each other.

dance sits up all night looking at the two babies as time sleeps and the early morning light finds dance sitting at the side of the bed still. when time awakens she finds dance's

-love you so much... thank you,

is all dance could manage to say before tears released and he
broke down and cried, for time had given dance the one
thing he'd never had... a family.

tearful eyes looking back at her.

      -love you so much... thank you,

is all dance could manage to say before tears released and he
broke down and cried, for time had given dance the one
thing he'd never had... a family.

                         ✳

twenty

in the path of time

as soon as folks hear of time's confinement there is the usual parade of well wishers and curiosity seekers who bring with them healing teas for time, food for the household and small gifts for the newborns. they would receive their real presents at their eight day naming ceremony. aunt affection and aunt cinnamon meet, greet and thank everyone on the front porch, guarding the entrance into the house and to their niece, grand-nephew and grand-niece as fiercely as watchdogs. it is a time for time to rest and the babies not to be disturbed.

it isn't until early the next morning that time gets a chance to really look over her babies in great detail. passage, as she would name her first born is perfect in every way. even at birth one could see the ebony features of dance chiseled on his face.

-ears just like his daddy's,

is one of the first observations the grand-aunts would make as they look for the tell tale signs of lineage and paternity.

-can see dance in that boy face each time he smile,

94

is another and it was true. his even temperament and quiet disposition were much like his father's as well. it seemed everyday passage grew more and more into a little dance. about his birth folks would jokingly tell time,

    –don't look like you had anything to do with him.

      –like you wouldn't even know one another.

      –just like a stranger you pass on the road.

        –like you waren't even there.

      –like dance had this baby all by hisself.

silence, as time would call her daughter, on the other hand looked like no one anyone had ever seen before. it wasn't just her lack of pigmentation, her pink eyes or her wheat colored hair, which grew wild upon her head. she definitely had the penetrating stare of her mother and there was something that vaguely looked somewhat like her brother but silence on the other hand looked like dance wouldn't even know her. that night time slept awkwardly as her rest was disturbed again and again by a face peering over the newborns in a dream which she was never able to remember when she awakened. if she had, silence would have seen the face of power replicated in the pigment-less face of their daughter.

aunt affection, always the eternal optimist, was convinced that the baby's coloring would soon come in. so each day when the grand-aunts came to visit aunt affection prayed as she searched for this illusive pigment. aunt affection studied silence's fingers and toes, hands, feet and ears for any trace of color she might have overlooked the day before. she tells time,

> –i's known chil'ren who took as much as three year to get they full complexion,

trying desperately to convince herself.

> –always comes in from the 'tremities, color does,

she says to no one in particular. aunt cinnamon replies,

> –hmmph! pretty baby but still look white to me, all over!

passage and silence share the exact same rhythm, they wake and fall asleep together. in many ways it is almost like taking care of one child, twice. they are good babies though. time loves her offspring, especially silence, not just because she is a daughter but also because she is the smallest and therefore most vulnerable. time worries because silence never cries. she seems to need to eat or be changed at the same time as passage, almost as if he cried for the both of them.

time continues on and the children grow stronger. as the period of her confinement comes to a close and spring emerges, time is anxious to return to the crossroads. this is the cause of the first real fight between time and dance.

-absolutely not! don't see what could be so god-damn important out at no crossroads that you got to sit out there with the babies all hours of the day and night. just don't make no kind of sense! don't want my children raised on no god-damn roadside!

time had never seen dance truly angry before and his request for an explanation had no answer she could give. since the moment she first heard the voices of the near born time was totally in tune with both babies waking or sleeping but she no longer heard other people's thoughts. it was as if in giving birth she exchanged the jungled cacophony for the solo of passage and silence's newborn harmonies. she had grown comfortable with this ability and although time loved her babies, she did not consider this a fair trade. standing on the porch nursing in the stillness of nighttime she receives nothing on the wind. time feels blind after such sight. time figures if she returns to the cross-roads her gift might return as well but there was no way for her to explain this to dance who is not in the frame of mind to hear it.

the news of time's premature delivery of twins arouses a slow stir within the little rural mountain village community but the birth of a

- 'bino,

causes quite a simmer. there are the ignorant who think that time had lain with some white man and brought his baby home to dance as well as the so called educated who think it is massa's blood resurfacing. then there are the spiritual that believe time cursed for misuse of her power, when actually it is power's misuse of time at issue. there are the cruel and heartless that think since time is blessed with a healthy son the cursed child should be put down as one would do a sickly farm animal. an opinion held by fannie elizabeth, though she keeps this thought to herself and still the ever hopeful others who expect miracles from the colorless child and look towards the sky for confirmation of signs.

the early birth of the babies resurrect talk of men time had known before marriage, although people are careful not to speak of this in front of dance. still dance catches wind of some rumor. as an unchecked fire underneath an untended kettle is bound to spill over, so it is with innuendo. eventually it gets back to time and although it could never be proven she had reason to suspect that fannie elizabeth orchestrated the events that lead up to dance's hearing.

dance stops by the little general store in town on his way

home to buy some of the peppermint balls time so truly loves. as the sun sets dance is greeted cordially by the men who sit outside on the store porch socializing every evening after planting during late spring and summer. although usually a tight knit and closed community, folks around town genuinely have taken to dance. he minds his own business, keeps basically to himself, works hard, folks can't abide laziness, is polite and generally very pleasant. for the most part they feel time made a good match. dance waits for franklin to count out ten fat peppermint balls from the jar on the shelf behind the counter when fast-assed rita and her best friend melva jean saunter up. rita has had eyes on dance since he first came to town and takes every opportunity to wind her hips back and forth whenever in his vicinity.

-how do mr. dance?

-how do?

melva jean echoes rita.

-sure is hot!

the two women chime in together. rita laughs. dance gathers his candy bag and drops two coins on the counter for franklin. he acknowledges the two women as he heads for the door,

-miss rita, miss melva jean,

and he keeps stepping. dance had no time for ideal chit-chat and was anxious to get back to his little family, besides he instinctively recognized rita as the trouble she was.

-uhmm, mr. dance?

begins rita, clearing her throat,

-how is miss time and her babies?

-just fine, thank you for asking,

dance responds.

-how old are they now?

-seven months, yesterday.

-seven months already, imagine? how time does fly. two babies must be a handful and you's still just newlyweds yourselves.

rita smiles, pleased with herself.

-you be sure to send miss time our regards,

adds melva jean.

-yes be sure to tell her we asked about her and her babies,

and with that the two wind their way down the road. within earshot, melva jean screams,

   -girl, don't believe you! callin' them time's babies.

breaking into a malicious laugh, rita responds loud enough for dance to hear,

   -girl, gotta call them time's babies cause truthfully they
   could be to anybody's... mama's babies, daddy's maybe...

and the two break into a cackle, whooping and hollering their way down the road away from dance.

it was not in his nature to listen to idle gossip and goings on so dance chooses instead to ignore it. dance alone knew time had been a virgin when he had taken her. it took him more than the better part of an hour to penetrate her as gently as he had. dance trusts in the love of time and although ignorant to the ways of women is sure time had lain with no other man and yet now on his way home there is a small rain cloud on the horizon of his mind in what had been a perfect day.

✳

twenty one

in the path of time

all during the autumn of her pregnancy time gathered wild-flower seeds. with the last thaw of winter she plants and patiently waits until the end of the rains for shoots to break through surface. by the beginning of may buds shyly begin showing themselves, still time waits but as soon as the first flower fully blooms time gathers her babies and some quilting squares before defying dance's wishes by returning to the crossroad. it takes some doing, what with transporting two small children but time had stood the imposed silence and exile of home as long as she could. it is the first time since giving birth that time ventured anywhere other than to church, the first time she and the babies had been out from under the watchful eyes of aunt affection and aunt cinnamon and the first time she openly defied dance.

that day at the crossroads time hears not a sound on the wind. time found she could no longer listen in on the passing thoughts of strangers. no one came to visit and she passed no one on the road. it is almost as if she has been put in quarantine. the silence is so deafening time begins to think maybe dance's hidden powers have orchestrated this absence of activity to demonstrate definitively his demand that time remain at home. the babies are fussy and time gets little sewing done.

it is the middle of the afternoon when time looks up, surprised to see aunt affection and aunt cinnamon's bad feet coming up the road. she had not heard either approach. their sudden appearance solidifies the reality that whatever power she might have held while pregnant had definitely gone. dejected in her loss, time never realized the gift was never really hers, only a result of heightened senses during pregnancy. she had only benefited from silence's presence in her womb.

in the approaching distance time could make out the aunts fussing long before they arrived at the crossroads,

-told you we'd find the heifer out here!

time hears aunt cinnamon's voice first, huffing with an effort to keep up,

-what in the world could she be thinkin' bringin' them
babies all the way out here?

time knows how upset they are for sure when she hears aunt affection reply,

-it don't make no goddamn sense!

time is shocked. she could not even conceive of aunt affection,

-takin' the lord's name in vain...

if time hadn't heard it herself she would never have believed it.

-suppose somethin' was to happen to you way out here?

aunt affection begins as soon as they get to where time is sitting on the blanket nursing the babies.

-sometimes wonder if you got the sense the good lord done gave you...

aunt cinnamon continues,

-baby girl what was you thinking? what would happen if god forbid one of these babies or you got sick out here, what you gonna do?

-we's all right,

begins time, but the aunts cut her off.

-all right? that's not the point!

-all right!

nearly screams aunt cinnamon,

-what if a snake was to bite you? god forbid. what
if you was to fall down and twist your ankle, how
you gonna get these here babies and yourself home,
did you ever think?

-and you might leave a note so a body would know
where to look for you at.

chides aunt affection, shaking her head.

-didn't nothin' happen. i's fine, the babies fine and
obviously you two didn't have no trouble findin' me.

-no thanks to you.

-heifer!

time could see the genuine concern in their eyes and hear
the worry it in their voices and she loved them for it.

-i's sorry. didn't mean to worry you but just had to get
out of that house for a minute, had to breathe.

they have already packed up to begin their rag-tag exodus
back to the farmhouse when aunt affection suddenly
remembered the strange man she had run into.

-there's somebody lookin' for you,

she begins.

-lookin' for me?

-well actually he in town askin' for the crossroads where
the quilt woman be at?

-what he want?

time asks, intrigued.

-how should i know?

-well what you tell him?

-din't tell him nothin'.

-why not?

-cause i din't know the man, besides which he ain't
ask for you by name.

exasperated, time says,

-but you knew it was me.

-no such a thing.

-but you just told me,

replies time, exacerbated.

-din't think of it to just now...

-now you just ought to stop all that lyin'!

jumps in aunt cinnamon,

-you knew full well that man was lookin'
for baby girl.

aunt affection says nothing.

-you knew full well!

repeats aunt cinnamon. aunt affection glares at her sister.

-...and you sat up there in church just yesterday!
ought to be 'shamed of yourself.

-well i din't know for sure,

aunt affection defends herself, rolling her eyes.

-he could have been talkin' 'bout anybody. besides, i ain't
hardly in the habit of giving strangers my business.

-usually you can't keep your mouth shut besides it waren't
your business, was baby girl's,

aunt cinnamon mumbles something under her breath.

-wonder who it could be? what he look like?

asks time, curious.

-like a stranger!

and with that aunt affection closes her mouth tightly, fixes
her face, sets her jaw, gazes straight in front of her and walks
on ahead. time looks to aunt cinnamon who just shrugs her
shoulders and shakes her head.

-when she get like this she impossible. always been
spoilt... can't call her on nothin'. like she the queen
of sheba or somethin'. like she the onliest one that
ever could be right! hmmmf! i pays the old heifer
no never mind.

there is little more said on the way home. the aunts don't
stay long after they get time and the babies safely in. as they
are leaving, when aunt affection offers her cheek to be
kissed, time attempts to apologize. aunt affection stops her
and softly sucks her teeth,

-no need baby girl. anyway it ain't you, it's that heifer,

referring to aunt cinnamon,

            -that owes me the apology.

   -and you just keep on waitin' for it, you hear? hell will
freeze over first, mock my word! always so damn sensitive!
wouldn't get hurt, all you got to do is just speak the truth,
            then you can walk with you head held high!

and with that aunt cinnamon turns, stretches her neck and
walks on out the door. time stands and watches from
the porch as the two aunts go down the path, angry, not
speaking, one in front of the other. time wonders again
who this man who knows her as the quilt woman is. she's
determined now more than ever to return to the crossroad.

dance is quiet when time tells him of her day. she decided
that it was best if she told dance rather than have him hear
it from someone else. there is no argument or fight this
time as she had expected.

   -why you bother to tell me? don't need my opinion,
            obviously gonna do 'xactly what you want.

dance finishes eating and sits out on the porch whittling
away at a piece of wood. he has no more to say for the
evening and time feels a distance grow between them. that
night, for the first time, dance turns his back to her in bed.
time is up two or three times during the night with the

babies and does not hear when dance arises. when she awakens dance had already left for work. it was the first time dance had gone off without kissing or saying goodbye.

it is overcast and the sky threatens rain. although she very much wants to, time decides against going to the crossroads and instead stays home. despite herself time is disturbed all day. in the period of her confinement growing wildflowers had become a passion. it started as just a bed of flowers around the side but slowly grew and now wildflowers sur-round one whole corner of the house and patches of wild-flowers could be found across their land. when aunt affec-tion comes over late that morning without aunt cinnamon, she finds time on her knees planting seeds in her garden. as time works aunt affection sits and watches the children sleep on the porch.

it is sometime in the middle of the afternoon when aunt cinnamon comes down the road with a tall middle-aged black, black man at her side. time, aunt affection and bernice are stringing beans on the porch and the babies are both sitting up playing with fingers and toes. aunt affection glowers down at her sister as aunt cinnamon introduces the man from the yard.

-baby girl, this here man done come looking for you.

the man, dressed in clean overalls and cap, looks to be about six feet or so, has deep set eyes, a salt and pepper beard and

wide arrogant nostrils. when he takes off his cap he reveals
a bald spot in the middle of his head. he holds his cap tightly in his hands as he looks up at time and begins speaking.

-you's the quilt woman who be at the crossroads?

time nods her head slowly, trying to figure out who this man
is and what he could possibly want from her.

-so sorry to disturb you at home like this.

-how can i help you?

time asks.

-don't rightly know. you see, you come to me...
in a dream.

aunt affection cuts her eyes at her sister.

-a dream? don't understand.

-neither do i 'xactly...

the man hesitates.

-you say a dream? what sort of dream?

-well not 'xactly a dream, more like a... vision.

111

aunt affection raises an eyebrow and clears her throat.

-you see i's been right poorly here lately with my health.
layin' sick, doctor says i's dyin'. been layin' 'round for nigh
on two week, runnin' a fever. couldn't hardly keep
anythin' down. was goin' in and out and at one point
'member seein' a crowd of people 'round me. could hear
voices and babies cryin', then there's this storm, thunder
and lightnin' like never seed before. suddenly it very quiet,
thought had died. in my dream i's covered in a quilt, kept
safe and dry. when come to i's well. that night dream that
i sees this woman sittin' at a crossroads, makin' the same
quilt that's 'tected me and knows i has to find you.

time is flabbergasted by his tale and silently shaken. she
doesn't quite know what to say. the two sisters exchange
glances and shake their heads.

-how did you know where to look for me at?

-gets up, starts walkin' and trusts my inner sight
to lead me.

aunt affection shoots another look down at aunt cinnamon.

-was waitin' by the crossroads when your aunt come by
and was kind enough to show me the way here.

aunt cinnamon looks defiantly back up to her sister.

-so sorry but don't know what it is i can do
for you mr....?

-they call me blue, blue river.

-well don't rightly know what it is i can do
for you mr. blue.

-well, main thing i wants to do is to come and
thank you.

-thank me for what?

asks time, timidly.

-for help savin' my life and wants to ask if i can buy
that there quilt,

and he points to the quilt folded across the banister to air
that time had finished just that morning.

-that there be the quilt i seed in my dream,

and although time denied knowing anything about
blue river's recovery, news of his testimony spread. that is
how the story comes into being, folks believing time's quilts
having healing powers. time continues quilting as always
and at the finish of each quilt another someone new always
showed up looking for the quilt woman of the crossroads

and claiming the new work. they all find their way to her, to sanctuary and they almost always have a similar story. there is the woman who claims in a dream time's quilt across her face brought back her sight. another woman, baby on hip, claims she had been barren until a dream in which she conceived on a quilt time had made. still there are the two sisters who believed each other dead until they meet at the crossroads, both drawn by a dream of seeing each other wrapped in a quilt of time's. they always came to buy the quilt just made. it got so time had only to sit at the cross-roads after finishing a quilt and wait for its' story to be revealed.

they bring of what bounty they have. some who could brought coins, others a bushel of corn, cabbages, blueberries or whatever fruit or vegetable happened to be in season, once two large apple cobblers and a great big pound cake, chickens, hogs, livestock of any kind, even a particularly beautiful scrap piece of lace someone might happen by and just knew time would love and could find a special place or use for.

as years pass by and her reputation grew there were even a few dollar bills from white-folks who somehow found their way here. dance doesn't quite know how to deal with time's newfound celebrity but has little to say. dance chooses to watch, listen and wait.

blue river stays around sanctuary and about six months later returns carrying two wooden rocking horses he had carved for the twins. they are exquisite works and although the babies are just beginning to walk and still too young to ride, they fall immediately in love with both the rocking horses and this blue river.

✳

twenty two

in the path of time

the children grow as is their nature. before anyone realized it second birthdays were upon them and then third and by this time everyone had gotten use to their strangeness. silence has gained no color, still utters not a sound yet it seems she and passage are in constant communication. they could be in different parts of the house and anything said to one seems instantly known to the other. dance first notices it when passage, sitting on the porch, spills his lemonade. silence is in the kitchen with her mother. dance reaches down to start wiping up the mess when in comes silence with a second cup for her brother. it becomes more apparent after passage talks. he could be in one part of the house and know exactly what it was silence needed or wanted to communicate from another.

time is a good mother. she watches her children like the so called hawk. never out of sight, children have a way of standing there one second and suddenly disappearing the next. time walked away from the twins to talk with her sister-neighbor at the edge of the property. time found since the wind's silence at the children's birth, she enjoyed the company of women-folk more, motherhood providing the bridge. time looks, passage and silence are playing at the top of the hill, near the running-wall separating time's land and her neighbor's, collecting wildflowers growing out of the spaces in the mosaic rock wall not thirty feet away from where she stood. both children inherited their mother's love for wildflowers. time turns around again to find passage bringing her a bouquet and silence kneeling down observing a line of black ants busy transporting a torn leaf towards the colony. when passage reaches time she thanks him for his flowers then turns around again... silence is nowhere to be seen.

they look everywhere. the child is simply gone. time nearly loses her mind. it is impossible, this disappearance makes no sense and does absolutely nothing to mitigate the insanity time feels closing in to claim her. there is nothing for silence to be hidden under, nowhere for her to go. behind the low rock wall the land slopes softly and one could see for a quarter of a mile.

time is panic-running in ever widening concentric circles screaming silence's name. time turns to passage and asks him where his sister is, even though he had been standing right next to her when silence vanished and she knows he could know no more than she. time did not expect an answer so she doesn't pay attention at first when passage answers,

-in the water.

it is the kind of non-sensible answer adults accept from children. passage repeats,

-in the water. silence in the water,

and points towards the brook down the red dirt road. suddenly time thinks of the well, making no logical sense. time never leaves the well open and there is an unobstructed view back to the great tree in the yard. silence would have had to pass right by her. never-the-less time begins running back towards the house.

her sister-neighbor is calling out, waving her arms and running up the path with blue river at her rear and even from this distance time could see he was carrying something. suddenly time realizes it is silence in his arms. time changes direction, fighting to hold back the scream she feels standing at the edge of her reason. suspending all thought, time grabs up passage and races towards her other child. silence looks up and time allows herself to begin to breathe again. only as time takes the child in her arms does she notice silence is totally soaked, head to toe.

without any understanding time turns to blue river, thanking him for silence's return. in the better part of an hour that silence has been missing, time had aged. it is this day she credits as the beginning of the silver streak that eventually grew to meet the iridescent lightening across her face.

-miss time, sittin' on my back porch studyin' on a
stump of purple heart finds me in the woods back of my
house last week, when hears me this splash in the creek
below. first off don't pays too much attention as snakes
be chasin' possum in this heat. somethin' feels strange
tho' so goes takes me a look and there stands little
silence in the water, just as still as could be.

isn't until time has silence at home, bathed, every inch
checked, fed and had lain both children down that she
remembers what passage had answered,

-in the water. silence in the water.

although she just put the children down, time goes back in
to check on them and from that day never again feels totally secure. when dance comes home that evening he does-
n't kiss time. very quiet, dance doesn't play with the children as usual. time knows he has something on his mind.
time has learned it is best to wait until dance decides to
speak. after the children are asleep for the night, dance
begins.

-what's goin' on here time?

he asks quietly, the story of blue river's rescue reaching
dance's ears before he even made it home. time looks up
into the questioning brown eyes of dance. dance sits back
and stares into time's face. there is a long silence. time does-

n't know exactly how to answer him. there wasn't anything she could say which would satisfy him, time really had no answers herself. all she could do was relate the series of events as they unfolded. she does. dance sits there and listens.

dance had been tolerant of the many people who came to seek time's quilts and attention, overlooked the rumors of supposed clairvoyance and never spoke a complaint after time resumed her trips to the crossroads but now this insanity was engulfing his children. instinct to protect his young overwhelmed him, something carried from across waters, something basic, a safe guarding of what god had entrusted, a part of manhood slavery couldn't strip away. watching freedom and miss margaret die awakened a place in dance he recognized as dark and foreboding, ugly, which he knew had to be kept in check, a primal intangible in danger of overflowing with a fury that dance himself was only barely just becoming aware of.

✳

twenty three

in the path of blue river

blue river builds a small wooden cabin down the road from time's land, right at the water's edge. he lives quietly, never bothering a soul. few folks know exactly where blue river keeps to himself. now in this part of the country folks like their privacy fine but find it necessary, now and again, to visit with society. not so with blue river. once he finishes building his cabin he only comes into town to buy supplies, about once or twice a year and doesn't attend church or spend any time around the men-folk at the store in town. he doesn't find the company of people appealing and well satisfied with his own, is never seen in the company of a woman.

once his small vegetable and herb garden comes in he is almost totally self-sufficient. blue's river's needs are simple, his dietary habits basic. he fishes occasionally in the brook behind his cabin and other than that blue river is never seen eating flesh. hadn't been for his woodwork he might have gone totally hidden within the landscape and among the unknown.

on his back porch is where he worships, the only word to call this relationship blue river has with wood. it isn't just the first class craftsmanship but the love expressed through his hands. when he works wood it is nothing short of miraculous. people need to touch a river piece, usually believing the wood to be warm or soft. folks say as they come upon a new work,

> –see you've got a piece of the river.

once word gets out blue river is kept busy with orders for tables, chairs, chest of drawers, cutting boards, kitchen stools and any other wooden object folks could find use for, orders blue river would fill. he so rarely leaves his little house folks eventually venture out to his back porch to place an order. it is then blue river builds the little shed, which houses all his finished pieces. blue river would make anything for you except a coffin, you just had to find him at home.

blue river makes his living in furniture but lived for his angels, his small sculpture pieces that sustain blue river's soul. years go on and blue river's back porch becomes proliferated with small wooden figurines, all angels and all colored. his angels seem to breathe they looked so alive. touching one of blue river's angels always made you feel better and upon occasion blue river would give an angel away,

> –as the angels dictate,

he explained but no matter how often asked or how much

money offered blue river never sold an angel or gave one away to white-folks.

> -would be like sellin' someone in my family,

blue river tells all those interested in buying one of his heavenly host. blue river thinks to himself but never shares aloud,

> -and ain't sendin' them out to live with no
> white-folks neither!

although later there would be a demand, blue's,

> -river angels,

as they grow to be called, are never for sale. many years later in that region if you were lucky enough to have a river angel in your house, it was thought to be blessed. over time it was said that river angels,

> -have power, bringin' to those to whom they belong
> whatever needed and to those who pray whatever
> they dream.

sitting out on his back porch working on a small purple heart angel is how dance finds blue river that next evening when he walks down after supper. dance carries one of time's berry cobblers which she baked when dance told her he planned to thank blue river. having had no need to wander, it was the first time dance had ever been this far down off the road. he feels at home as soon as he lays eyes on the small wooden cabin, it reminds him of miss margaret's. caught off guard, he fights back an almost uncontrollable urge to cry. dance gathers himself and continues down the sloping path towards the water's edge and the wooden cabin. he finds blue river on his back porch humming a little tune and working on a piece of wood. so engrossed in his task at hand blue river does not notice dance's arrival. dance stands and watches, not wanting to disturb blue river's concentration, mesmerized by the quality of the workmanship and his sheer speed. blue river is carving the wings on a small purple angel. although the face is angelic there is a surprising scowl and a look of annoyance from the figure. dance has never seen anything so compelling and never the experience of a piece of art reaching him in this way. blue river puts down the small carving instrument, seems to come back from a great distance, readjusts to returning by focusing on objects around the room and finally sees dance.

-evenin' dance, you been standin' there long?

-evenin' blue, not long.

-sorry, when i's workin' don't see much of anythin'.

-it's all right, enjoyin' watchin'. never seed anythin' like it before. where'd you learn to do that?

-been doin' it all my life guess, since a child.

dance suddenly remembers why he has come.

-oh, this here for you, some of time's berry cobbler. little
somethin' to thank you for yesterday.

-very kind of her.

he dusts off wood chips from his pants and stands to take the
dessert from dance.

-please take my thanks back to miss time, waren't
no need. didn't do anythin' but carry the child home.

-anyway we wants to let you know how
appreciative we are.

-excuse my manners, dance please take a seat.

-thank you blue,

uncharacteristically, dance sits, totally comfortable on blue
river's porch listening, within seconds lost to the bubbling
song of the brook waters. blue river returns with two hunks
of the cobbler set in deep, dark mahogany bowls with
spoons carved from the same wood. there is no way for
dance to refuse. he feels totally relaxed, sitting here eating
as with an old friend. after finishing eating the main event

125

becomes the magnificent setting of the sun over the blue mountains. it is so reminiscent of a time spent within the quietude of miss margaret's company that dance had all but forgotten. dance returns to his childhood, revisiting its' ending. being awake and seeing his fire nightmare carries dance to his feet. with the revisiting of these memories the eighteen years chasm threatens to resurface as he stands on the verge of remembering. it is as if a door finally swung open and dance suddenly faces the abyss he'd wandered. he slowly begins to negotiate his mind's eye through a wasteland, barren of any conscious participation in this life. there are only glimpses at first, flashes of colors, images jumbling one upon another, out of context and without reference.

dance remembers wet and cold. he is drenched. he isn't sure if he has fallen in the water or been caught in a torrential downpour… standing facing a large cedar tree on a small hill. does not know for how long he's been staring down at the large exposed root system, mesmerized by the intricacies of the great tree's root as it goes deep into the earth, interweaving around itself in an almost incestuous embrace… standing on a low bank watching a small stream of foam coming up as water rapidly breaks over rocks and stones… squatting down, water cascading over his buttocks… just before sunset and a flock of golden butterflies flying around his head… extremely cold, standing in the mouth of a cave staring out at an emerging sunrise over a small canyon covered in the frost of a late winter's snowfall…

flashes keep up all night, only just beginning, it takes the better part of a month before dance is able to piece together some of the missing years. the one image he sees clearly in all his confusion is the back of freedom leading him when he could not lead himself.

dance looks up and sees the night grown deep in blues with indigo corners and realizes he has been here without speaking for at least three hours. he looks over to blue still holding the same angel he had when dance walked up, sanding as he did every evening. blue river finds in the dark a grace, as his fingers work on their own. blue river looks up and nods to dance as dance's eyes refocus on the present. no words are spoken as none are needed. slowly dance stands to begin for home. the two men say,

-goodbye,

recognizing the kindred spirit each has found here. there is a stillness within blue river appreciated and returned in the quiet dance. blue river knows few people who do not disturb his space or his work. before dance leaves blue river reaches over and taking a small soft cloth wraps the angel he's worked on all night and quietly hands it to dance.

the new moon is barely visible, playing hide and seek between the clouds. by the time dance reaches the road it is hidden and the night dark again. it is then dance notices the glow from underneath the cloth covering the wood.

dance unwraps his angel, realizing not only is it giving off light but a certain amount of heat as well. taken with the luminescence found, he stands there marveling for a while. slowly looking back before turning, dance begins to walk home, a river angel for company.

✳

twenty four

in the path of time

it was dusk and a welcome unexpected shower lasting no more than three minutes pushes the august heat up off folks a bit. in those first ninety seconds the vocal persistence of god sends all living creatures seeking shelter. the inherited stupidity of cows is overcome as even bovine search for cover. in those second ninety seconds the passionate fury of heaven's might reigns supreme as all beings of breath and light come to a halt, fearful to move less they be detected by the raging power in the sky.

time is standing on the front porch watching the children play. dance has built a swing for the almost eight-year-olds, suspending two leather seats on twine rope hanging from one of the great branches of the mighty tree in the front yard. silence and passage sit there for hours staring into each other's souls as they rock away. if time or dance couldn't find either child in the house they usually found them facing each other on dance's swing. they only swing together, never alone. for passage and silence it is a shared activity.

it has been a quiet afternoon and time's dinner's cools on the stove. she's fried up some of the fish dance brought back from blue river's brook early this morning and spent the afternoon making half moon apple pies for the picnic the church holds once a year out at the park. she always made half moon pies, apple filling set in a circle of dough folded over. time leans against the railing, tasting a piece of lemon pound cake she is sure aunt affection's going to bring. always been her favorite, since a little girl. time finally sent the children outside when she couldn't stand their helping hands anymore. covered in flour up to both elbows, she returns to the kitchen and places the last batch into the oven. she could hear peals of passage's laughter as silence and he twist and unwind again and again on the rope swings.

time calls the twins in at the first sound of rumbling. with the initial drops of rain passage lets out a squeal of pleasure as both children run towards the house. dance is rushing up the road. when they see him they both break into a frenzy, veering away from the front porch towards their father. passage and silence race, arms open, towards dance as they always do. laughing, he nearly drops his sack running towards the children. by the time dance reaches the yard it is already dark, the kind of darkness usually associated with cataclysms or sometimes accompanies fast moving eclipses of the sun. what happens next is something no one could ever exactly explain.

what was most striking is it is one of the only times anyone could remember when the twins moved out of tandem. for some reason silence suddenly turns, as if hearing her name, runs and stands before the great tree with her back to everyone. throwing back her head she opens her arms as if asking to be picked up. silence takes a deep breath, opens her mouth and lets out a first sound, a scream or more like the high pitch dolphins sometime make.

dance and time stop, their baby had broken her silence. only god knows how dance has suffered or how often time had fallen to her knees to pray for release of the yet stilled voice of their child. in all the years, until today, silence had uttered not even a whisper just as she manifested not an iota of pigment despite aunt affection's continual chagrin.

they have no chance to celebrate. silence looks up, time follows her gaze just before a tremendous piece of lightning hits near the top of the tree alighting a branch and setting the ancient tree aflame. time gasps as she runs towards her child. silence, in what seems to be slow motion, rather than moving further away from the tree moves closer. suddenly silence throws her arms around the trunk and in plain sight, standing at the base of the burning tree, silence slowly disappears. there are merely seconds between the lightning strike and time's arrival at the intertwining roots. time grabs into the vanishing mist but silence is not there.

dance stands holding passage who closes his eyes tight and would not reopen them. running to the spot where silence left, time and dance stand there staring at the tree, at the sky above and at each other.

                    -no! no! not again!

is all time kept screaming over and over for the better part
of the next three days. time couldn't believe it all seemed
so familiar, like a dream of suffocation from which she could
not awaken.

※

twenty five

in the path of dance

aunt affection and aunt cinnamon keep vigil, looking after the needs of passage, dance and especially time, fending off the visits of the purely curious while continuing to illicit the help of any neighbor willing to look for their grand-niece. they coordinate the plates of arriving food and the companionship of sincerely concerned women-folk who sit and keep company, usually sewing or knitting as their men-folk formed search parties and combed the surrounding areas. aunt cinnamon feeds dance and the army of beleaguered troops searching for the missing mute while aunt affection watches over time, sitting at her bedroom window sleepless, staring ceaselessly at the burnt tree trunk which testifies in the front yard and over passage, who has not spoken, eaten or opened his eyes since his sister's evaporation and whom time would not let out of her arms for more than half a second.

the elders maintain a hopeful front but when the second day draws dusk without sign of silence hidden thoughts of a community, demons of silent accusations, begin to surface.

-children don't just disappear into thin air...

by dawning of a third day the search party dwindled down to nothing. dance sat all night on the porch. impatient for the sunrise he gets up and goes to look in on his wife and son before stepping out to renew his search. he has no idea where he is going but dance knows he cannot rest until his daughter is found.

aunt cinnamon is sitting up in the large chair in the living room, in her apron with her head tilted back, snoring in a deep, heavy sleep. a long thin line of saliva running from the corner of her open mouth, hangs down from her chin terminating on the back of one of her ancient hands. dance is struck by how old and wrinkled her hand is and realizes just how hard this has been on all of them. suddenly overwhelmed, the hope he has hidden himself behind begins to crumble, threatening to come down in ruins. dance slowly slides down the wall reaching for the floor beneath him. once he hits wood there is no getting up, his vision blurred by tears of utter frustration and once again the impotence of his freedom. dance begins to emit this whine so softly aunt cinnamon at first isn't sure where it's coming from. so many years after having walked off the slave farm still something could come steal his silence and he could do nothing to stop it. dance sobbed. men cry so ugly. broken, he rocks there crying for he has no idea how long. it is a touch of someone's warm and comforting hand on his back he next remembers. that hand reaches all the way inside the place dance has retreated to and eases the torture of his tormented troubles.

-it all be in the hands of god, child, no matter what we chooses to think. put all yo' trust and faith in him. he the onliest one can see you thru the trials of these here troubled waters.

dance hears miss margaret's voice asking him to,

-listen for the answers,

through aunt cinnamon's wisdom.

-you has certain gifts. it is within you to find this child. jus' listen!

dance's eye catches sight of the river angel on the corner table. he reaches over and kissing aunt cinnamon lightly on her cheek, walks through the screen door and off the porch. without saying a word dance turns and begins walking down the path towards blue river's.

blue river is working on a new angel out of blue soapstone. there is a rock bed not far from the cabin. he's walked by it many times but this morning he heard a voice call out so clearly he could not pass. usually he works in wood some-how deeper pitched, he hadn't thought of it before but male in gender he supposes but for the first time the voice is almost distinctly feminine. blue river had finished the out-line of the body and wings but the angel still had no face. he stops to make breakfast and finish cooking a pot of vegetable soup on his wood burning stove. even though it is the middle of the summer, blue river loves his vegetable soup for breakfast. he had just sat down to soup and a slice of pan fried bread when he hears the splash in the brook. he stands up and there is silence, soaking wet, climbing onto the bank. blue river runs down towards the child. this is the second time silence has returned to him. blue river gets the girl up to his cabin porch and goes in to get a blanket when dance appears at the top of the hill. it is hard to explain the emotions which erupt when dance sees silence standing on blue river's porch... relief, confusion, anger. dance begins to run.

the first thing dance notices as he approaches is the one set of wet footprints from the brook and up the steps to the porch where he finds silence soaking wet, cold and shivering. blue river hurries through the door, time's quilt in hand. the two men look into each other's eyes for just a moment. blue river wraps the blanket around silence and leads her over to the table. silence stares at the soup and bread.

-you hungry child? go ahead, eat.

silence does so, ravenously. the two men look to each other again. dance has not spoken, he just keeps staring. over the last few years he and blue river have become friends. questions ride into cognition but remain just below formulation. dance realizes he doesn't know what's going on but in his heart he feels blue river couldn't hurt any child. it is at about then dance hears time's yell of,

-silence!

ring out from behind them. dance turns to see time, with passage leading the way, followed by aunt affection and the hobbling aunt cinnamon in tow. when silence catches sight of passage she brightens up and holds up both arms, he does the same. silence would have run off the porch if dance had not picked her up into his arms and held her. he instead wraps the child back in her blanket and starts walking down the steps toward the running time.

time looks into the eyes of dance with such gratitude there are no words. she kisses her child over and over again and again as she checks for bruises, breaks or any signs of abuse. totally spent after the reunion of touch and tears, the tattered troop trudges homeward triumphant.

-how did you know?

dance asks time as they walk up the path.

-it was passage.

dance looks down at his son who keeps step with his father while staring into the eyes of his sister.

   -all of a sudden he opens his eyes and sits straight up,
silence comin' home. she in the water, silence in the water
now! he grabs my hand and starts pullin' me sayin', come
on mommy, we gotta go get silence. and all the time he's
pointin' in the direction of blue river's… that what he said
the last time, that silence was in the water… dance, what
that man want with my child?

dance stops, turns to look at time, then at silence who has
fallen asleep on his shoulder.

     -your daughter return home to him.

on the porch dance transfers silence to her mother's arms
and sits down in time's rocking chair, frightened by the level
of fatigue which accompanies his every movement, he connects to the times of his life before when weariness of life
was as heavy as his eyelids told him he was at this moment.
dance barely stirs when aunt affection and aunt cinnamon
take their leave and once again when time puts a quilt
around him hours later but not enough to awaken from
dreams in which he watches blue river standing at water's
edge holding silence. he starts to run but no matter how fast
he runs towards the water the two figures only get further
and further away.

✳

twenty six

in the path of cinnamon

-the child found in the waters 'round his cabin...

-but where she been at for the last two days? that's
what i like to know.

-say she come thru the water?

-the water?... well, what that mean? what water?

-they say the child was wet and that this ain't
the first time!

-wet? what you talkin' about, ain't the first time?

-girl no, seem like the child went missin' before and
guess who found her?

-no! oh, now that's just ugly!

-where the man come from anyway? he ain't from
'round here.

-don't nobody rightly know, just shows up one day. ain't

never hear him takin' up with anybody.
living out there all by yourself? it ain't natural, tell you.

-well, did he touch the child?

melva jean turns to fannie elizabeth and gives a large
significant sigh and rolls her eyes,

-well, told you they say the child was wet when dance
come upon them... if it true they needs to run the man
out of town.

-wet? why the child wet? that's what i don't understand.
did he bathe the girl?

-no, told you, say he found the girl in the waters...

-what waters?

-at the edge of his land. say she just come out of the
waters, from nowhere, all by herself.

-and where was he, when she was doing all this
appearin' out of?

-supposedly sittin' on his back porch. say he just sat down
to breakfast when silence decided to wade in... again.

-this a mess!

in a town as small as sanctuary the evaporation and reappearance of a small mute albino girl is cause for conversation. hard to keep such goings on out of the mouths of folks as questions appear in the consciousness of a community unable collectively to come up with a conceivable explanation to bring the entire affair to conclusion. instead left to their own devices they try and bring comprehension, allowing their imaginations to soar. most, upon hearing the complete story, simply thought blue river a conjure man of extraordinary powers or accused him of trafficking in the dark arts and dealings with the devil. suddenly silence is attributed all sorts of powers. there are those who still believe she should be put down, others who are sure time and dance are in league with blue river, that they have somehow given him their daughter or lost her in some commerce of souls.

even aunt affection and aunt cinnamon get into it. it's sunday morning and silence has been home for more than a better part of a month. instead of abating, talk about silence begins taking on epic proportions. by now almost no one retold a version of the story even remotely resembling the facts as they had occurred. everyone in town had their own interpretation of the events and through retelling the evaporation and return of silence begins the slow journey from gossip to tale to legend. so it really should not have been a complete surprise when at breakfast aunt affection makes the mistake of common speculation before aunt cinnamon. all she said was,

-curious, isn't it sista, how out of nowhere, all of a sudden passage just starts talkin' about silence comin' out of the water? he practically led us right to his sista.

aunt affection says nothing for a while as aunt cinnamon continues to eat her bowl of fruit salad, giving it full attention.

-after what the child say, can understand why baby girl walked to blue river's... but what i don't understand is how dance knew to go down there first.

aunt cinnamon stands up suddenly and pushes her chair away from the table. she brusquely clears away her place.

-wonder why the child keep endin' up out there, with that man?

aunt cinnamon sucks her teeth and rolls her eyes.

-and where the man come from anyway? told you not to bring that man to baby girl. ain't been nothin' but trouble ever since. say he hold some kind of influence over dance and...

aunt cinnamon cut her off. she takes the plate she is

142

washing, raises it above her head and brings it down with all her might. it shatters into a thousand and three pieces. aunt cinnamon has red fire in her eyes as she spits out a venomous reply,

-heifer, how is it you can stand here on a sunday mornin', dressed, ready to set foot in the lord's house and bad mouth folks?... then got the nerve to call yourself a christian? don't understand. you, of all people, knows how much baby girl and that boy love them babies?

then aunt cinnamon crosses to stand across the table from aunt affection with a look of disgust that is palpable and in muted dulcet tones as she might to a child,

-that boy family. he part of this here family.
family don't cross family. no one love his family more
than dance and lord know baby girl ain't the easiest to
live with, much as you done spoilt the child.
so quick puttin' the bad mouth on somebody... did you
ever think to yourself how come the child always choose
to return herself to that man out there? she don't come
back to your old rusty dusty behind, now do she?!
as much as you dote over her, she don't reappear sittin'
on your old ass lap, now do she?! and as far as i can see
mr. blue ain't been nothin' but neighborly, upstanding and
christian. all i know for sure is all the christians ain't
in the church.

aunt cinnamon cuts her eye at her sister and says purposefully,

-everyone talkin' 'bout heaven ain't going to heaven and everyone sittin' up in a pew ain't a christian. say the church where the devil do his greatest work. just thank god the child able to find her way back home. didn't baby girl say herself she and dance both seed the child disappear? so what, you believe baby girl got somethin' to do with it? didn't you hear passage say,

-silence in the water?

-he in on it now, too? just listen to yourself, you ought be shame. judge not, less you be judged and bear no false witness... you needs to go down on your hands and knees and pray the good lord's forgiveness!

cinnamon had never talked to the elder affection like this before and affection was not used to being spoken to in this manner. although and probably in part because she knew cinnamon was right, affection couldn't keep herself from saying,

-you's the one i blames for bringin' this mess into baby girl's life, heifer, you... blue river! told you should of left his old crusty ass behind out at the crossroad where you found him but no! you the one invited this trouble into the house...

came to me in a vision... woke up and i was healed...
        let my inner sight guide me... negro please!
            bible say the only way the devil come
            into your midst is you invite him in.

the two sisters suddenly find themselves locked in a combative embrace, rumbling and tumbling around the kitchen in their sunday going to meeting clothes, gray hair and wrinkles just a flying. although they are both elderly, except for aunt cinnamon's bad feet, they are both in relatively good shape and very evenly matched. they roll and tussle around the kitchen for nearly a quarter of an hour before the younger cinnamon emerges sitting on top of her sister.

the result was the same as it had always been since childhood, aunt cinnamon would win, just barely but at such a price it was hardly worth the hard fought victory. aunt affection never gave up and always proved a bad loser. as the elder she felt she was owed respect which translated into doing everything her way. aunt cinnamon, only eleven months younger, knew many times aunt affection was just plain wrong. when aunt cinnamon lost fairly she was a good loser accepting her loss and moving on, whereas aunt affection always held on to the bitter end refusing to accept defeat and long past losing she still held a grudge. even now aunt affection continued to struggle,

                -get on up off of me.

after aunt cinnamon rolls off of her sister she sees the trembling lower lip of aunt affection as she struggles to get to her feet. looking around at the mess made, aunt cinnamon doesn't mean to but she does the unimaginable and begins to laugh. aunt affection stands over her sister, afterwards she could not have told you what came over her but she does the unpardonable, she spits. the clear spittle traverses the distance between them, still resonant with laughter and hits its' target on her closest temple, slowly sliding downward descending across cheek bone and following the line of the jaw to nearly the center of her face before aunt cinnamon reaches up with the ever present handkerchief residing at her wrist and slowly wipes.

without speaking aunt cinnamon gets up and with hatred stares into the eyes of her sister before she turns to wash and change. that morning the two sisters arrive at church at different times and for the first time anyone could remember they sit apart. from that day forward they are rarely seen in each other's company for in the time it had taken for that expectorated liquid to cross space and find its' mark, the sisters irreconcilably lost one another.

the crime proved unforgivable and from that day until the day her last remaining sister died, cinnamon refused to mention affection's name and never in this life would they ever speak to each other again.

※

twenty seven

in the path of blue river

granting grace is exclusively the prerogative of god, for without god there could be no grace. blessing in life is god's alone to give and only his to withdraw. to become ancient is merely to awaken within god's good grace each morning again and again. simply finding god is grace and in that moment lies eternity. purpose is many times revealed only on a need to know basis and so quite often one continues on one's path, clearly within hand and sight of god, without knowledge of destination. within this enormity, swept along as we all are by the tide of manifestation, only in the non-resistance of total submission can the pure nature and freedom of god's good grace ever truly be realized... with the greater gift also comes a greater power and of course a greater responsibility.

blue river was a truly natural man. intuitively he understood his place in the universe. blue river never remembered parents, only others about him. blue river doesn't rightly know how old he is. when he comes into his consciousness he is alone. found and raised on the land with the cree people until their forced migration, everything he has, had been given him by nature and blue river trusts in her divinity. he had been taught there is much to learn from every one of nature's creations. blue river recognizes god's work in the softness of a cloud swept sky or the lover's embrace of wind in the arms of an adolescent tree, in the cooling breezes of a summer's night or the gentleness of first light. his was the gift of simplicity, for blue river had few needs and in this he was blessed. a quiet life within god's good grace is all he ever sought, no more. there is such a great gentleness in god's grace that it's easy to take for granted. paradise so easily lost when white men came with their dead eyes, which lied, and their plagued blankets which killed. grace so quickly withdrawn. as happens so often in life, one's path is altered irrevocably, in the way a river shifts course and is changed forever. it matters not that the river should want to retrace its' steps for there is no return for rivers. rivers flow in only one direction and with the exception of the obstinate nile, always towards the heat of the equator.

blue river outlived everyone he knew. when small pox came he buried his baby son before his two daughters and then his wife succumbed as much to her grief as to the insidiously virulent viral strain. in a cave blue river lived quietly on the land. he went down to the burial ground each day and wandered alone amongst the dead, laid amongst their remains and at night walked amongst their ghosts until long after the sickness came. when he caught the fever he prayed to die. either god did not hear or refused to listen for blue river was graced with the cruel curse of immunity. blue river had always taken his responsibilities seriously, as they were revealed and applied himself as guided. trust and submission allowed blue river to now accept the tainted gift of his life, returned. it was time to start over again and so when the pull to the waters of sanctuary began it was not within his nature to refuse. blue river received a call. summoned from his sick pallet just beyond the edge of death's encampment, he had as little choice about changing course as any other river and once diverted, a seemingly insignificant degree in a mountain stream's slope may lead to cascading falls over cavernous depths. there is never any reason looking back for rivers only flow in one direction.

at sanctuary lay hidden a pathway to sacred waters. chosen gatekeeper, without his knowledge or consent, blue river was entrusted and its' ancient entrance placed for safe keeping in his hands. what better way to keep a secret than not to even let the secret keeper know there is one.

-on a needs to know basis...

he still knew little of his purpose here but he had been brought to sanctuary, led to build his cabin at just this spot on the water, just as the songs of his river angels were real. this was why blue river could reach in and release the angel-spirits, which called to him. when blue river took his sunrise walk each morning he was led only by the voices he found within fallen branches and discarded tree stumps dis-covered along his way. listening to the call of a bird as he arrives at a fork in a road might determine which direction taken as a falling apple might indicate the best place to rest, the buzz of a bee impending hazard or a rush of birds reveal time to move on. blue river's solitary life proved satisfying until the second time silence came through the waters. whatever little peace he had found was shattered after that. he knew folks thought he had something to do with the child's disappearances. he felt their stares.

> -the child come thru the waters? what kind of
> nonsense is that?

he had seen it himself. he had no idea why the child returned herself to him but there did seem to be a bond. although it had been time's quilt that first brought blue river, it was silence that kept him here. from the time he first laid eyes on the child blue river knew somehow that silence was the reason he had been called from the near dead. he didn't know exactly how but he knew somewhere their destinies intertwined.

※

twenty eight

in the path of silence

     -**a**m almost five when da-da appears. he's come
before, when i's a baby, before i 'members good. the next
time i's playing with passage near the big tree when i hears
    him call my name. way inside i knows his voice and i
turns towards da-da. my arms reach out to be embraced.
    lifted way up, folded into the center of his caress,
i feels warm and 'tected. the sky raises and i am in this
kind of yard and all these men's hitting on these drums
and women's dancing, some singing and some beating
on these gourd like things. can't see too good for the
brilliance. my eyes adjust to the light. 'member a great
savannah. standing on a hillside inside a cathedral of blue
mountains, surrounded by herds of black and white baby
    goats all around. i wanders off from his side and am
    somewhere i ain' 'posed to be. it nearly sunset.
      within the thunder and lightning hears
          him call my name.

              -a-che

he calls me again,

              -a-che

it mean power. it my ancient name, in the tongue of
ancestors. it means the same as his...

this is the place from before. here i can speak. i am no
longer silent.

passage awakens from his dream.

✳

twenty nine

in the path of dance

blue river sits on his porch and watches the sunrise. it is a peaceful morning but had not been so yesterday, a day, which dawned similarly. he had sat admiring the same sky and having his morning bowl of oats and stewed fruit when dance and a group of men came down from the road to his porch. he watched them, sensing something in their quiet manner both mean spirited and menacing. blue river sat still, in the way of the people, continuing to eat. he slowly put down his home carved wooden spoon as dance stepped up onto the porch.

-mornin' dance.

-have you seen my daughter, blue?

-no... she gone missin' again?

dance didn't answer, there was no need for the look of anguish in his eyes was enough.

-excuse me, blue... but i got to look around here.

-you's welcome to look anywhere,

blue said, indicating the surrounding land and the brook.

-in fact give me a moment to put out this fire,
come with you.

-got to look inside.

blue river stops and stares intensely into dance's eyes for a moment, dance hangs his head.

-said you can look anywhere.

blue river repeats softly. dance could not even look his friend in the eye.

-she my child,

dance spoke softly. blue river opened the door wide and sat back down to finish eating. he did not allow the tear, which formed, to fall. quietly blue river echoed,

-you can look anywhere,

dance repeated hollowly,

-she my child.

that was it. so gently the bonds can break. so delicate is the knot of trust that without it the rope of friendship could not remained tied. of course silence was not in the small one room cabin and when dance emerged alone he knew what price he had just paid.

three years had passed since the last time silence reappeared. in that time the relationship between dance and blue had grown. it had not been difficult for they really enjoyed each other's company. so alike in many ways they had grown close enough to know the thoughts of one another. that was why dance could not look up into the eyes of blue river because he did not want to see the hurt he would find there. the bond between the two men after this was forever damaged and dance's shame reflected in blue river's eyes.

when they saw dance return to the porch without silence the men moved on but their suspicions lingered. dance still could not bring himself to look at blue river. it nearly broke his heart when he heard,

            -care for some breakfast, dance?

all he could manage to do was wipe away a falling tear as he shook his head and mumbled in the negative. as he stood at the top step he heard blue river say from behind him,

        -dance, hope you know i would never do anythin'
                to hurt your child.

his vision blurring, he began to walk down the stairs,

a simple,

                                 -i know,

was all dance could manage...

                       ※

thirty

in the path of time

silence is gone for about a week. this time though is different, there is no sense of panic, almost as if she had gone on an extended sleep over and expected back in a couple of days. this faction led by aunt cinnamon whose one comment to time was,

   -child found her way back before and she much younger. she'll find her way home again.

time takes comfort in this though she keeps passage close by. it is passage's comment that gives rise to the most excitement though when he announces,

      -silence with her da-da.

this sends aunt affection to bible to read over and over again the passage,

    -thou shall have no other god before me...

    -from the mouth of babes...

is aunt cinnamon's reaction when she hears what passage

said. raising her right eyebrow, she cuts a quick eye at her niece who continues staring out the window and detecting no reaction aunt cinnamon instead watches passage. on the seventh morning aunt cinnamon gets what she has been waiting for. suddenly just after awakening, before using the slop jar, passage announces,

-silence comin' home today,

as soon as he finishes his obligatory bowl of oats with raisins and honey, aunt cinnamon has him by the arm and out the door. time is not far behind and aunt affection, never one to be left out, follows. passage travels the same route he had taken three years before. she hurries him along for this time she wants to see the returning. she pays no mind to her feet, heavy as they were, so excited over the prospect of witnessing a miracle. of course aunt cinnamon recognized the inherited miracle in the drawing of breath and in the certainty as to which direction the sun would travel. she was not unmindful of his many blessings and the place they have in everyday life. she didn't mean to sound ungrateful for she appreciated even the miracle of color spread out before her eyes at this particular moment but it had been a long time since something qualifying as a

-bon-a-fide miracle,

had come her way and she didn't intend to miss it. aunt cinnamon was pleased to arrive at blue river's before the blessed event. although breathing hard, she came up the porch stairs as she would the deacons row on communion sunday when anticipating a firebrand pastor. she greets blue river as she hits the top step with a resounding,

-mornin' mr. blue. my grand-niece comin' home. now ain't it a glorious day?

-it is a magnificent mornin', miss cinnamon, that fo' tru'. sure glad to hear about your kin-folk. that silence sure a slippery one, she do travel some.

-she hard to keep up with, that the tru'.

-any idea where she be at when she...?

-your guess be good as mine. only the good lord knows and he ain't seen fit to confide in me.

-hmmm, well she sure couldn't of picked a mo' beautiful day.

-yes lord, ain't that the god's honest tru'...

-mornin' mr. blue.

-mornin' young man. how are you? seems you grow about an inch every time i sees you! boy you mus' be eatin' up everythin' in sight. great day in the mornin'!

if you don't look the spittin' image of your daddy?
like two peas in a pod, i swear.

a big smile comes over passage's face. blue river excuses
himself as soon as they are seated. he has some bread in the
oven that needs coming out. by this time the water has
heated. he makes cups of peppermint tea, sweet and brings
out one of the hot loaves of bread to cool with a knife and
a jar of honey he collected yesterday. he and passage eat
themselves silly, devouring most of the loaf and a second cup
of tea before fully satiated.

time, on the other hand eats nothing. she sits staring out at
the waters of the brook which runs behind blue river's cabin
and waits. she has never noticed before just how quiet and
peaceful it is out here. it's almost summer and everything in
bloom. the regeneration of the woods and life eternal that
replenishes itself every spring returned with its' usual
vengeance. although it is nearing eleven o'clock there are
still shadows and spaces where the first light has not yet
retreated so consequentially there are still birds singing
morning songs. the trees around blue river's cabin are filled
with the activities of nature. time listens to their melodies
and finds herself enchanted. it is one of those breathless
spring days when summer peaks though. nature is full to
brimming, air thick with the nectar of life, where an entire
world waxes and gives birth while all which lives upon the
planet is reborn, again.

they settle back to watch the passing day unfold. throughout its' course, the surrounding hillside becomes a stand of
watchful eyes intent on witnessing a miracle or disproving
one. folks come in ones and twos as the word spreads of
silence's anticipated return.

as the morning wears on time watches blue river work. outside of dance no one has seen blue's river angels before, with
whom aunt cinnamon finds an immediate affinity. from the
blue rock he is sculpting she watches an angel slowly
emerge, almost as if blue river is aiding and abetting the
angel's escape as he carefully chips away the outer shell
exposing the hidden angel buried within. the angel seems
to practically climb out of the rock and engage her. the
river angel was perfect, this time could see as blue river
holds up his work to the sky to scrutinize it. the angel stands
just under a foot high with a wing span of about half of that.
there was something about this figure that made you want
to reach out to it. time couldn't help herself. it was smooth
and once in her hands, time found the angel warm to the
touch. while she held the angel she sensed this wave of calm
wash over her and with it a feeling of well being. holding
the angel, all worries seemed to fade. upon careful exami-
nation she found the angel perfect in every way except for
its' eyes. there were no pupils, instead empty sockets. time
realizes the angel is blind. time notices a change in herself.
there is the absence of panic that accompanied silence's
other disappearances. there is almost a sense of surreal calm.
time knows somehow in the place where silence is she will

not be harmed. time feels possibly in the presence of miracles and despite herself jealous of her own child.

dance joins them just after noon and as folks arrive with food the event takes on a festive atmosphere. folks bring blankets and instruments. aunt cinnamon is coaxed into giving a rendition of,

-down by the river side.

it is the first time blue river hears aunt cinnamon sing. she has a beautiful voice. blue river takes out an old blues guitar he's had for ages. when blue river was a young brave he traded skins for the strange sounding instrument, determined to learn how to play. over the years he played with anyone who sat by his fires to trade. by his second life he'd mastered the box of talking strings. folks totally mesmerized, aunt cinnamon and blue river sing and play for hours. sometimes occurs a marriage between instrument and voice so striking one could no longer suffer to hear either separately again. this was the case between blue river's guitar and aunt cinnamon's voice. there was nowhere either could climb that the other could not follow and yet neither seemed to lead or lag behind. perfectly matched side by side through melodic changes and chord progressions their souls seemed to soar.

when they finish blue river hands aunt cinnamon this one angel, sitting on a tree limb that caught her attention. marveling at its' detail and apparent warmth, the angel is over-weight, tired and seems to need to sit badly. her eyes are cast downward and aunt cinnamon is sure she is looking towards her tired feet. the sculptured piece had totally drawn aunt cinnamon in and she almost missed her miracle.

passage, who had fallen asleep, suddenly awakens and announces,

-silence comin' through the water.

those are the words that time has been waiting for and without saying anything quickly gets up and walks to the edge of the brook. at first time sees nothing, her keen eyesight detecting no movement and then there appears a seam and emerging through it silence, walking out of the water, stepping up to the bank. the transition seems effortless, somehow easy. one minute she is nowhere then suddenly there she stands peering into the dusk. silence would have walked passed her mother if passage had not called her name but by this time, time was paying more attention to where silence emerged from. time could not help it and found herself wading into the water at the place silence had set foot on shore.

blue river stands on his porch and watches this strange relay as mother takes daughter's place in the water. he watches time wade into the brook until she is finally in to her shoulders. he watches her submerge her face and finally her

entire head in an effort to find the point of silence's
reentry. folks stand stock still. a total silence falls upon
the gathering and then suddenly folks are all talking and
moving at once. the entire crowd rushes towards silence,
nearly scaring her back into the water. blue river has a
blanket waiting and has kept the pot of water boiling for tea
but the only thing silence seems aware of is the river angel
blue has been carving all that morning, sitting, waiting for
her return. almost imperceptibly the angel calls out to
silence as soon as she sits down and she turns toward it. blue
river hears it, passage does not.

time stands out in the brook for nearly a quarter of an hour,
repeatedly sinking beneath the water in what appears from
the shore to be a strange self-baptismal. finally time calls out
to the elements,

 –leave her alone! why can't you just leave my child alone?

as she stands there time begins to cry.

there is no stopping of tongues and by evening this miracle,
witnessed by so many, serves not only to confirm the pre-
dictions placed upon the albino baby those many years ago,
it also confirms the innocence of blue river.

aunt affection is of course happy to have silence back but
devastated by the innocence of blue river. aunt cinnamon
feels vindicated although she does not gloat. throughout

the joyous subsequent celebration, aunt cinnamon neither speaks to nor acknowledges her sister in anyway. it could be said that the innocence of blue river marked the beginning decline of aunt affection's health as over blue river aunt affection lost her sister's company. well this wasn't true in the strictest sense for although cinnamon would not speak to affection they still shared the same house, same meals and family but affection had lost her sister's voice. cinnamon would not speak to her sister until she apologized. affection knew cinnamon was as stubborn as she if not more so. affection could not find the road to apology so she said nothing. the truth was in the hollow of her being aunt affection still felt there was something not right with this blue river. she never trusted the way he had just come along with that mess about dreaming time up. then this mess with baby girl's child going missing and always turning up with him.

-nobody ever heard of any mess like this 'til he show up. now the child reappearin', out of nowhere, right in front of his cabin... 't'ain't natural.

aunt affection tells herself once again.

-devil's work! no, this truly a mess,

and she would have nothing more to do with this blue river. unable to rectify these disparate feelings and finding herself slowly alienated from the closeness that blue river seems to usurp in her family, aunt affection keeps to herself more and more. she takes to staying in her room, sometimes only coming out for meals and water. aunt cinnamon notices,

-maybe the heifer will learn some humility.

aunt cinnamon, who after nearly seventy-two years is truly over her sister, feels aunt affection's despondence but refuses to offer any comfort.

-not until she apologizes... or hell freezes over first.

that night there is a celebration at the home of time and dance. aunt affection bakes two of her spectacular lemon coconut layer cakes and prepares a huge jar of ginger sorrel. not to be outdone aunt cinnamon fries six chickens and put together a large batch of potato salad. the neighbors who helped look for silence come with their children and a dish, before long time's yard takes on a festive air. wildflowers adorn a large makeshift table and folks sit out under the full moon and have themselves a good time. there is of course non-stop conversation about the goings on down at the waters. there is speculation about blue river's power, the power of silence and the power of the waters. no one speaks about the power beyond.

time sits on the porch with silence and passage at her feet. she would not let them leave her side. silence held onto the angel blue river had given. silence remained transfixed on the bluestone angel and could not take her eyes off of it. the blind angel made a gift of itself to silence and so blue river gave it to her. silence had since not let it out of her grasp and even as she fell asleep held on tightly to her river angel.

✳

thirty one

in the path of time

by the next afternoon's arrival there was little else spoken of besides the reappearance. there are those who share aunt affection's suspicions and do not fully exonerate blue river,

-after all who is he, anyway?

-and where he come from?

-don't nobody seem to know? ...what kind of name is that anyway, blue river?

-livin' all the way out there, by hisself...
ain't natural.

-say he don't never carry no woman out there...

-never?

-somethin' ain't right.

-ain't natural i tell you.

-wonder what he do with that little girl way out there?

-say the girl ain't been touched.

-what would you say?

-say the girl walked right on out of the water and that blue river ain't had nothing to do with it.

-they say christ walked on water too... believe what you want.

the story winds its' way on down to dean's barbershop where the men-folk gather around to listen to the radio, then across the road to the women-folk buying groceries and finally home with the children from the school yard to their mothers hanging wash and serves as conversation for every supper table that evening. there is no way to keep the,

-reappearance,

off their tongues. rita and her cohort melva jean can't get their fill of details. rita just about winds her hips off as they pass dance on the road, intent on finding more gossip. dance for his part is never anything but exceedingly polite if not condescendingly civil. paying rita no never-mind, dance tips his cap as he crosses the street. rita, not accustomed to the charms of her magic breasts and hypnotic hips having no affect on any man she aims to cap-ture is baffled by dance's continual refusal to take notice of the many advances she lay in his way. it only seemed to fuel

169

her determination. simply because she cannot have him rita craves dance more.

  -you look like a lovelorn puppy every time he glance in
      your direction. right pitiful, if you ask me...

chides melva jean. stopping to admire her shape in the drug store window rita bemoans,

      -what does time have that's so goddamn special
                that i don't?

              -dance,

howls melva jean, who then can't stop laughing for nearly an hour. every time she looked at rita's angry face she got choked.

          -it ain't all that funny.

            -so you say...

laughs melva jean again. rita is burnt and thereafter even more determined to get dance into her bed. whereas before she threw her charms in his pathway just whenever she happened upon him, now this became a full fledged campaign. to pass time she draws up strategies in her head. she allows herself to think about the prize at the end of this journey, dance but not too often for she finds it too distracting. rita formulates plots that allow her to come into close contact with dance as often as possible. she maps out his comings and goings as she contemplates his betrayal. this is not easy, dance, a man of habit and strong convictions, has shown absolutely no interest in her. what she does not undrestand is that dance finds rita and her whole crowd somewhat vulgar.

sunday she studies her prey. rita gets to church early and watches aunt affection and the little girl, aunt cinnamon and the little boy and then dance with time on his arm, walk in, their eyes fixed directly in front. they sit, as they do every week in the seventh pew to the left of the preacher. from her seat on the back row rita could see the back of dance's head and some of the blue hat that time had sitting up on hers'. rita tried to bore holes into the back of that blue hat and wanted to rip the little piece of veil hanging off of it. time gives no attention to the looks and stares of rita. she is totally unaware of her existence that morning. time has her eyes firmly fixed in front but only so they could keep on her daughter. time now tended to become watchful and suspicious of everything and everyone. she begins to look at blue river differently, the affect of hearing aunt affection refer again and again to her distrust of the man taking toll. time also feels the added pressure of being the center of attention whenever she is out, especially with silence. they now only leave the house and its' surrounding lands to go to church. that morning the minister chooses to preach his sermon on jonah in the belly of the whale and his journey home. the

similarities to silence are not lost on anyone in the congregation, especially time who feels that the business of her
family had become sermon fodder. she views it as a breech
of privacy. rita notices the way time's neck sits up straight
as the young reverend falcon makes his way through jonah's
ordeal and towards his return to dry land. time is sure that
every eye is on them that morning. as they leave the church
rita sees her opportunity. reverend falcon always conducts
the benediction from the rear and therefore everyone has to
pass him on their way out of service. the congregation bot-
tlenecks on the front steps while the minister greets each
parishioner. dance and time, each holding on to a child just
reach the reverend falcon when rita sidles up, interjecting,

   -how upliftin' the sermon was this mornin', reverend.

rita looks directly at silence and then innocently into time's
eyes,

    -seems we've got our own little jonah right here,

then brazenly to dance,

     -the lord do work in mysterious ways,

time sends her a look, cutting her eyes.

      -his wonders to perform,

calls out the reverend falcon with spirit, in his effort to save the situation. without even looking in her direction, time speaks softly,

> -there was one about the temple and they called
> her jezebel...

taking dance's arm she looks into the face of reverend falcon and smiles civilly,

> -good day reverend.

the family turns and begins walking down the red dirt road, dance holding the hand of passage, time the hand of silence and the two grand-aunts behind, side by side, neither looking at nor speaking to each other.

from that day on there was a marked difference in time. she participated less and less in the goings on of the community and became for the most part a recluse to all but her family and close friends. she tries also to keep silence and passage as close as possible, especially silence. to the outward observer it might appear that this is the concern of a over protective mother but the truth lie closer. time wanted to study her daughter to discover her abilities. although time witnessed both silence's departure and her return she still had a hard time accepting what she saw. time was jealous of

her child, the celebrity generated and also of the relationship she suspected between silence and this power from
beyond.

✳

thirty two

in the path of dance

dance is aware of the changes in time but says nothing. he, better than anyone, understands what time has been going through. the next morning he awakens to find time standing in front of the tree that silence had been taken from. she walks around and looks up at its' burnt branches. then she strolls around it to take in another vantage point. time suddenly collapses against the tree. dance hurries from the upstairs window believing the strain of silence's disappearances caused this emotional outburst. he was wrong, time cried because she couldn't find the entrance to reach beyond. she thought if she stood in the same place silence had been taken from the entrance would be made clear. it wasn't. by the time dance reaches time she is sobbing uncontrollably. he holds her until the shuddering ceases then he helps her back to the rocking chair on the front porch.

time withdraws further and further. she no longer sits at the crossroads. all she does is watch her children. when they sleep she works on her quilting and stares at the tree. since silence's last disappearance when dance reaches for time at night she pulls away and in the mornings is already up sitting in the children's room. her whole day revolves around silence and passage. time has always been a good mother but now she never lets them out of her sight.

dance begins to worry when he comes home for lunch and finds time with the children down at the tree. time has silence by the shoulders, yelling and shaking her. all dance could make out was time saying something that sounded like,

> -the door, where's the goddamn door?

> -what's wrong, time? what's baby girl done done?

dance asks, as he picks up the child to comfort her. silence throws her arms around dance and buries her head into the place where his neck and shoulder meet.

> -she just willful!

is all he gets out of time, who turns and walks off leaving dance holding a tearful silence. passage stands a little ways off. his eyes large as he stares at his sister and then at the back of his mother's diminishing figure. of course passage knows, there is nothing silence keeps from her brother. they are still able to look into each other's souls with the ease of thinking thoughts of their own. he knows of the man she calls da-da and also of the extraordinary place she journeys to. passage knows at least as much as silence does of her strange travels. time though never thinks to ask passage who feels no compulsion to share.

-time... time!

dance calls but his wife chooses to ignore him and instead quietly walks up the steps closing the screen door behind her. dance doesn't like this. he looks at the door, looks at the crying silence in his arms and looks into the eyes of his son. passage offers softly,

-mama want silence to show her the way.

-the way?

dance asks, unable to believe what he is hearing.

-what way? the way to what?

-all she say is, where the way? where the goddamn door!

dance's eyes close until they are little more than slits. dance finds himself fighting to breathe as if suddenly his nostrils can't intake the amount of air needed and he finds himself breathing through his mouth. he struggles to calm himself as he sets silence down and follows time. dance finds time in the kitchen rolling out dough.

-what the hell wrong with you?

she looks up and spits dance a look, rolling her eyes. it is a look intended to tell him to back up and give her some room. unfortunately dance is somewhat blinded by his own anger and continues in towards time. all that happens over the next few seconds is still unclear to anyone who hears the story and still somewhat unbelievable to those who witnessed the event. dance is furious. time feels threatened. no one notices the children follow their father into the house. dance steps toward time. time swings the rolling pin catching dance squarely in the side of his head. dance goes down like a sack and lies there without moving on the floor. time turns. passage stares in disbelief at the prone figure of his father but silence stares directly into the eyes of her mother, the look of hatred palpable across the small distance of the kitchen. time stands with roller in hand. silence looks through the flour slowly sifting down and fights to hold her mother's eyes, a visual embrace neither will soon forget.

time seems to stop as she waits for dance to move. surely she had not meant to kill dance, just back him up off her. thankfully sometimes it is the intent which god hears. finally dance begins to twitch, involuntarily. he lingers in a coma for three days, during which time dance is visited by miss margaret who sits by his bed and nurtures him as she had done those many years before. dance is her greatest work and she is not about to lose him yet, at least not this way. miss margaret knows her time on this side is nearly over and just as she is about to fade away she gives her last magic, bringing dance through, again.

when he sits up that evening and looks directly into the eyes of time it is a different being she encounters. dance recovers or at least most of him does but he is never the same. there is nothing about him physically one could see that was different but the changes that occurred were profound. dance never spoke of the incident but he never forgave time. there is a distance that dance wraps himself in. that day he looks at the tree in the yard, still huge despite the destruction of the top and makes a decision. the next morning time and the children awaken to the sound of pick ax on wood. they find dance attacking the great tree in the front yard. time begs him to stop,

-dance, what in the name of god has gotten into you? let that tree 'lone. it been standin' in this yard longer than any one of us can remember.

dance pays absolutely no attention to time and continues to swing away at the great tree. no amount of pleading or cajoling alters the swing of his ax. when she had exhausted all other reasonable arguments time lets fall,

-you can't take a chance it's the doorway.

dance stops and looks at time.

-...in case silence needs to go back.

-she don't need to go back.

dance looks at time in the hoodoo way. he studies and allows his eyesight to blur slightly in the way he was taught. dance catches a glimpse of time's soul exposed, an all consuming jealousy and it is as if truly seeing her for the first time. she believed it wasn't fair that silence who couldn't speak should be blessed to travel across the veil and still unable to tell anything of when she returned. dance understood now that time closely watched silence so she could follow her daughter across at her next calling.

dance returns to his task with renewed vigor. it is mid-afternoon when the giant tree cries out as it falls. it is early evening before dance finishes trimming the branches and chopping the elder tree into smaller lengths. there would be plenty of firewood this winter.

time refuses to speak to him. when dance comes in there is a covered plate on the table. time had not called him in for dinner. she retired early. dance refuses to eat. this strained silence continues for a while. dance never takes food again from time and never again reaches for her either at night or early in the morning. he begins to eat his meals elsewhere and for the first time dance notices other women.

things finally come to a head about a week later. after work dance goes into town to bring home some licorice sticks, which he knows the children love. he thinks of bringing home some peppermint balls for time too but changes his mind. dance runs into bob and roy washington, one married to and the other still the unknown lover of fannie elizabeth. dance always found the brothers comfortable. they were farmers and their lands lay adjacent to one another. together they owned the largest piece of farmland anywhere within fifty miles, yet when the washington brothers approached you in the street they were just regular. whenever silence went missing they were always among the first to offer their assistance. standing there talking in front of the general store the three men find a common bond. fannie elizabeth is pregnant again and both brothers feel the strain, inducing a need for a night out and dance for the first time that he could remember did not feel like going home. the three men are enjoying the evening and each other's company. roy, the bigger of the two red-boned mountain brothers suggests they go by the honky-tonk out behind jackson's old quarry where they serve moonshine. they trek off to the little one room shack. when they arrive dance could not believe how much reminds him of miss margaret. whenever he enters backwoods it is almost as if he could feel her walking beside him. once inside the roadhouse shack he soon forgets the comparison.

dance is not a drinking man. in all the time that dance has lived with time he never drank. it takes him a few drinks before he suspects and a few more before he is convinced, dance likes to drink. dance is a quiet drunk. in fact the more he drank the quieter he became. this was fine for in compensation the more the washington brothers drank the louder they got, so they never noticed the change in dance. when bob and roy were ready to leave he wasn't. by then dance had no intention of going for there was something much more pressing on his... mind.

melva jean, rita's friend was sitting alone smoking hand rolled cigarettes and throwing back shots of moonshine when dance and the washington brothers arrived. she had been waiting for rita who stood her up, probably for the

-fine dark new hand at the quarry,

she's had her eye on. melva jean laughs at the irony. here sits rita's precious dance across from her favorite table on the one night rita chooses to be absent. this humor is not lost on melva jean, especially as dance stares at her breasts continuously throughout the night. when the brothers leave dance sitting at the table alone, staring into his fifth drink melva jean knows it is time to go over and reintroduce herself.

-may i sit down?

dance nods his assent and melva jean slides down.

-i'm melva jean patterson.

-i know.

dance is quiet.

-never seen you in here before.

-never been.

-what brings you out tonight?

dance smiles. melva jean notices how he quietly runs his eyes over her body.

-aren't you gonna offer me a drink?

-you want a drink, melva jean?

-well, that's not what i really wants.

dance looks into melva jeans eyes.

-so melva jean patterson, what is it you really want?

she looks dance up and down slowly before she licks her lips.

-for you to walk me back home.

dance looks at melva jean. after what seems a small eternity passes, dance suddenly gets up, gathers his cap, throws back his fifth cup of moonshine, pays his bill, puts his arm around melva jean's caramel colored shoulders and proceeds out of the juke joint. other than his leaving with melva jean, no one would have ever suspected just how drunk he was. dance does not stumble and is almost deadly silent.

once outside she grabs his hand and dance follows melva jean meekly, a lamb to slaughter, to her small house at the edge of the woods on the far side of the quarry near the old railroad station. standing in the broken moonlight on the front step of melva jean's two room house dance allows himself to be kissed for the first time by anyone other than his wife. melva jean leads him to the small cot in the dark. dance allows her to take off his shoes and unbuckle his pants and pull them off. laying on his back dance gives no resistance, his engorged member providing melva jean with all the incentive needed.

late the next morning dance awakens, mouth dry, smelling of moonshine and melva jean. all he has on are his socks. dance had barely opened his eyes and gotten his bearings as carnal flashes replay from last night's encounter when there is a rap on the door. suddenly the door flies opens, sunshine flooding in and amidst the brilliant sunlight stands a silhouetted figure. before melva jean can fully awaken or dance move the figure speaks,

> -melva jean what you still doin' in bed, girl? the
> goddamn afternoon's half gone,

and in strides rita.

-girl, let me tell you about last night...

it takes her eyes a minute to adjust to the light. rita's voice trails off as she begins to focus.

-oh, so sorry girl, didn't know you had company.

rita actually turns to leave when the image of a naked dance, which her eye only glimpsed in the internal darkness, registers. she turns back again. she cannot help herself as she focuses on the mammoth rising that claimed dance each awakening since his thirteenth year. dance reaches for a sheet to cover himself, there isn't any. he can't find it or his pants, both balled up on the floor on the other side of the bed. melva jean is slow to awaken as rita stares, transfixed.

-dance...?

is all rita is finally able to utter.

-do you mind? rita? ...rita?

-...what?

she answers as if coming out of a trance. slowly she turns her head to look at melva jean.

-well, do you mind? could you give us a little

                                privacy, please?
rita still has not moved.

                        –please! i'll talk to you later.

regaining just enough presence to find her way to the door,
rita says as she steps back into the sunlight,

        –yes girl, can see we have a whole hell of a lot to
                        talk about.

rita could not help but take another look at dance's
standing member as she closed the door behind her.
dance and melva jean hear her laughter drifting in and out
as rita makes her way down the country road toward town
to tell anyone she could find.

dance turns to look at melva jean. he was not drunk now,
somewhat hung over but not drunk. the true realization of
last night's indiscretion settles in. before he can finish fully
processing the extent of the carnage that now lay in its'
wake, after all he hadn't even gone home at all last night and
missed all that mornings' work, melva jean, her incentive
revived, mandated by dance's arising nature, surrounds him
with her mouth. quickly dance evaluated that the damage
done far outweighed any possible consequences to taking a
little more time with melva jean and so once again as she
prepares to mount him, dance lays back, allowing the rest of
the day to slowly pass to dusk.

✳

thirty three

in the path of dance

dance had fallen out of love with time. this is the one thing he understands walking home that night. he hadn't gone with melva jean because he was drunk or stayed with her afterwards because he had fallen for her amble bust line but merely because he no longer loved time. there was something in the violence he had witnessed in her eyes just before she hit him. for a moment he was looking into the eyes of a caged wild animal. he couldn't reconcile that image with the woman he had married. arriving back home around dark, he is met on the road by aunt affection. when he gives his usual,

-evenin', miss affection.

she stops, turns to face dance and stares a hole right through him. her lips are tight and she utters not one sound. after a suspended moment aunt affection rolls her eyes, lets out her breath in a rush and steps past dance continuing on her way down the path. dance approaches the front porch. he could see silence and passage chasing fireflies in the front yard. at first he does not notice aunt cinnamon sitting, rocking. the children's race toward dance once he has been spotted and both give him hugs. he gives them the candy he brought for them the evening before. dance is silent as he climbs the steps. he stands noiselessly on the landing for

a moment before he reaches for the door. aunt cinnamon
stops rocking,

-well ain't you gonna speak to an old lady?

-good evenin', miss cinnamon. didn't see you's
sittin' there.

-evenin', dance.

-'cuse my manners.

-it's all right. know you got a lot on your mind.

dance turns and leans against the railing watching the children enjoy their treat. for a time there is nothing spoken
between aunt cinnamon and dance. finally he sits down on
the steps and allows his forehead to rest on the slats of the
banister.

-you must be hurtin' pretty bad boy...

aunt cinnamon whispers. she is not looking at dance but
studying the colors as they fade in the sky. dance has no
answer and so he says nothing.

-to hurt baby girl the way you done,

she finishes her thought.

-ain't tryin' to be all up in your business. know you
to be nothin' if not fair and know baby girl sometimes
ain't the easiest to live with.

aunt cinnamon gathers her shawl around her as she prepares
to leave.

-left you some dinner on the stove.

as she passes dance she grabs his forearm and looks him in
the eye.

-whatever mess you and baby girl into, y'all ain't the
'portant ones here now. it's them babies out there.

she pauses before saying intensely,

-it's them babies! do the right thing, you hear?

she squeezes his arm until he is almost about to yell out.
dance is surprised by the strength in this old woman.

-they didn't ask to come here! you understand? and if
they gets hurt you all will have me to deal with!

aunt cinnamon is all up in his face. dance is sure too she
would prove a formidable foe.

-do i makes myself clear?

she stayed right there until dance could feel the heat of her breath.

-yes, ma'am. perfectly clear.

seemingly satisfied, surrounded by the encroaching dark- ness, aunt cinnamon kisses the children and continues on down the road. even from a distance dance could tell how bad her feet hurt but only god knew the enormous weight of her sadness and he kept close her confidence.

✳

thirty four

in the path of time

if a cut is not properly cared for it will get infected. the most dangerous infection is the one which goes untreated. pus must be exposed to drain. even the smallest infection, if allowed to prosper will eventually kill the greatest of hosts.

time chooses not to speak of dance's absences which turn out to be more and more frequent. eventually she stops cooking for him altogether as it becomes apparent that he is not eating at home anymore. he would come home every evening after dinner and play with the children until time for them to go to bed. sometimes he would stay out on the porch and watch the sky but more evenings than most found him down at the road house shack tossing back moonshine. sometimes he would accompany melva jean home but most of the time he would sit by himself and get quietly drunk. something had changed in dance since time went upside his head with the rolling pin. love was so important to dance, though he never thought to speak of it. his love for time had been his anchor, he now felt adrift. he had lost the trust of goodness in himself and could no longer see it in other people. he resonated toward his lowest common denominator. dance simply was not happy.

this was a particularly bad time for the children. they could feel the strain between their parents. time was becoming more and more withdrawn from the world and dance, although he is there to put them to bed, was never there in the morning when they awakened. passage begins to suspect dance doesn't sleep there at all after he wakes up in the middle of the night to relieve himself and on his way back to bed peeks into his parents' room. only his mother is there. he looked all around the house and out on the porch, no where could he find his father.

meanwhile other changes are beginning for silence. just after the twins' ninth birthday silence begins her menses. aunt affection proves to be a god-send. her keen perception first notices the changes in silence. she had been looking for them, after all the woman in their family flow early, though she has to admit none quite as young as silence. aunt affection is at the house when silence gets her first blood and there when time speaks to her daughter. showing little interest or enthusiasm time perfunctorily explains to silence how to manage herself and her linens. this is a time when silence needs her mother and tries to spend as much time as she can around her. time couldn't move for silence.

> -go on, now! you don't have to be all up under me
> all the time,

is all she says. time does not know the affect her indifference has upon her daughter. silence feels rejection deeply.

it is aunt affection that provides the celebration of silence's passage into womanhood. she instructs silence on the do's and the don'ts while explaining the joys and complexities silence's new status in the community elevates her to. aunt affection explains to her grand-niece how women conceive. she has given this talk to so many young women before, then aunt affection bakes a serious chocolate layer cake. as they eat it with hot sweetened tea, aunt affection gives her a strand of tiny blue stones which she tells silence to always wear around her waist under her clothing to make any childbirths in the years to come easier.

the subtle changes of nature within silence have a profound affect on passage too. for the first time in his life he found a distance when he reached for his sisters' thoughts. they have always shared everything, lived every experience through each other. they provided reflection for one another, a synchronicity, one inhalation, exhalation the other in a tandem breath they both shared since before birth, until now. what was so devastating for passage is this detachment seemed to occur in the course of a day and he had no idea why. suddenly he found himself locked out and couldn't rightly figure out what it was he had done to cause this estrangement. it was his first lesson in the fluid nature of women.

time had taken to sleeping or really it would be better stated to say that time had taken to dreaming. wonderful dreams, elaborate intricate dreams that were all consuming.

she started taking occasional naps at first, just a brief one after lunch, then perhaps grab a few quick minutes before dinner. soon she was planning the completion of her day around sleep. she found herself going to bed right after the children, sometimes even before dance had gotten out of the house good. then she started retiring right after dinner, allowing dance to watch the children alone until their bed-time. eventually she begins taking dinner to her room. soon time is running the house from the bed, directing the children to perform one task or another like a rear commanding general. this she does in between her naps. she gets up once a day, to cook dinner. this takes a supreme effort and then one day time just simply does not get out of bed at all.

both aunt cinnamon and aunt affection find this situation intolerable. although they both speak about it to time they do not mention it to each other. their conversations with time are very different though. aunt affection chooses to question in quiet dulcet tones and comfort in non-demonstrative phases.

    -baby girl, wouldn't you like to sit outside in the sunlight for a little while? won't you eat a little soup? you've got to eat somethin'. you've got to talk about it sometimes. you can't hide forever. it's a heavy load but never more than we can bear... never more than we can bear.

aunt cinnamon takes a much different approach. she

doesn't believe in care by coddling. she storms into the bedroom and stands over time. speaking loudly, in clear ringing tones,

-baby girl, you ain't sick, so why is you up in this here bed? know this ain't over no man! know we done raised you with better sense than that and who you think s'pposed to be takin' care of your children while you layin' up? truth be told baby girl, you done done enough in your own way to help drive the man away.

for the first time in days time seems to return to the surface of consciousness. she shoots a look of anger at her aunt. aunt cinnamon happily notes the movement without appearing to do so and continues on,

-ain't no secret where the man be at. dance sittin' over there drinkin' at that shack they got built out there in the country not far from doke's still. say he layin' up with that no good melva jean.

time's face hardens but aunt cinnamon could see she was listening to every word.

-if you wants the man, go on up there and get him. if you don't, then get over it and on with your life...done fried some fish with grits, gonna go make the table.
hurry now, we'll hold lunch.
you ain't the onliest woman in the world to lose a man,

lord knows... and you won't be the last,

aunt cinnamon thinks of herself. what a different life she would have had if she had just gotten the chance to marry leroy. she hadn't thought of him in years until this afternoon. she could still see him working out in the field, tall, black, sweat shining off shirtless muscles rippling in the sun. she could still see his smile and hear his deep voice calling out,

-evenin' miss cinnamon,

tipping his cap as he passed her on his way home every night. he had asked her to marry him the night before he had gone missing, found hanging in miller's grove. of course no one knew what had happened or at least no one who would say. she felt a chilly breeze come up behind her as she finished setting the table.

what both aunts failed to recognize is that time's withdrawal from the world began long before and not as a result of dance's leaving. nevertheless after aunt cinnamon leaves the room time gets out of bed, washes, dresses, comes downstairs, sits at the kitchen table and eats,

-like someone with good sense,

observes aunt cinnamon. afterwards, time sits on the porch and watches the changing light of the afternoon until the approaching sunset. time looks around at her family, the two aunts preparing to leave, passage growing like a weed, already past her shoulder. she notices just how much he looks like his father. time thinks of dance and melva jean and her thoughts harden. then she turns and looks at silence. in contrast, she is barely growing at all. she too looks like her father, a face which seems to come more and more into time's dreams these last few days. she notices how silence is changing, rounding, becoming spherical. everything about silence seems to be in flow. when time asks for her to bring the comb and grease, commenting,

-lord, lord, just look at my child's head,

instinctively aunt cinnamon and aunt affection look at each other. they have each tried to do something with silence's hair but it defies all the knowledge held within their aging fingers and ancient hands. despite diligence and discipline, silence's hair refuses to be contained. it slithers out of braids, cornrows, bands or any other attempt to confine it and consequently just stands all over her head.

-every blessed straw-colored knap to itself!

had been aunt cinnamon's last comment on the subject. no one had ever seen anything like it, her hair simply refused to be imprisoned and to add,

-insult to injury,

silence had the unmitigated gall to be tender-headed. she would cry and squirm, fidget and turn until aunt cinnamon vowed to,

-cut it all off!

if she didn't sit still, promising if she had to deal with silence's head,

-just one more time,

that would be its' fate. the only one who had ever been able to do anything with silence's head was her mother and although neither aunt speak of it they are both encouraged to see time up and about and more than a little relieved that they didn't have to tackle silence's head again.

the real reason for time's warp is that she was beginning to remember being raped. revealing itself in stages, the day of the lightning strike haunted time over the years in her waking hours as she struggled to remember. there was something camped out on the edge of consciousness which she could not manifest into coherent thought. it was like a tickle, a private itch there was no way to scratch that would not go away. it wasn't until she began to dream for her daily activity that the clarity of the memory took hold in her mind.

after eleven years, one rainy night about a month before dance stayed out, standing in the mirror in the middle of her bedtime ritual, time had applied a mixture of plant herbs, aloe, cocoa butter and mineral oil and was beginning to massage the outline of the scar with her fingertips. the keyloid from the scar on her face after so many years had become so smooth and faint it was barely recognizable. the physical scar the lightning left over time actually came to enhance her beauty. the ethereal scar left on her psyche was far more subtle and devastating.

abruptly a crack of lightning rips across the night sky right outside of her window. before time could hear the accompanying clap of thunder time began suddenly falling backwards as she had those many years ago. in her mind she relives her encounter with power, fully awake. lying on her bedroom floor shaking, time remembers white sands and warm breezes in trees of an oasis. she recalls a two mooned purple sky and recaptures the ravaging face of power she has seen in dreams over the years and most frightening, time recognizes that face in her daughter's.

time lies there for she knows not how long. it was no dream. it makes no sense but she knows its' truth. in its' own way it brings some understanding for it explains her silence and why she looks like she does. for so long it had been disconcerting to time that she carried, labored and birthed two children and neither of them looked anything like her. they both looked like their fathers. when time finally manages to struggle to her bed she sits there in some sort of shock. time wonders if she has finally lost her mind and then at the same time knows she has lifted a veil that has surrounded her since the day the lightning struck. she does not sleep as she makes herself look again and again into the eyes of power which dance in her head. it was the only way she could remember and she wanted to fill in every detail.

she remembered the lightning strike and could now connect it to everything that occurred until her return. as she gently rocks, stroking the slightly raised scar with her forefinger, she remembers power pounding inside of her and the way she felt afterwards laying on the beach numb and shaken. again she felt used and somehow dirty. she couldn't decide which was worse, knowing or not knowing. time finds herself torn between feelings of anguish, fear and rage.

twice during the night she gets up to go into silence's room to stare into her daughter's face. she is changing, growing up. she looks just like her father and time feels something she's never felt for one of her own children, hatred. she is thankful that this feeling only lasts seconds before going. she now has an idea where it is that silence is taken to when she disappears. time understands, standing there in the doorway, that power is in her seed.

it's wonderful to be close enough to divinity to glimpse god's plan but sometimes we can be so badly mistaken when what we see is not god's work. the wisdom to distinguish between the two a by-product of grace.

finally, just before dawn, time falls into a troubled sleep. she dreams of bernice sitting at her table eating a large piece of blue trout off of passage's plate who is hand feeding her. a dream time doesn't remember. that next morning, after conscious memory reunites with subconscious, time finds herself traumatized by her past victimization and yet strangely liberated by its' knowledge.

✳

thirty five

in the path of time

dance sits on the porch for the better part of an hour enticed by the seductive smell of wildflowers before time and the children return. he is just about to get up and go look for his family when he recognizes the long strides of his son coming along the back trail that leads down to the brook and blue river's, followed closely by silence and her mother. they are getting older. even in the magenta light of the setting sun he could see in the tall lanky frame of his son the man he would soon become, his shoulders having broadened and his body hardened. passage, already taller than his mother, now comes up to dance's chin. it is like staring into a mirror, passage looks so much like a younger dance.

it's also as clear that silence is becoming a woman. dance watches the way she moves as she gingerly picks her way. in this light silence looks unearthly. her complexion seems to reflect the colors in the sky but even wrapped in a quilt her silhouette looks like her mother's had when dance first met her. silence has not grown nearly as tall as her brother or even her mother but even in this light it would be hard to mistake her for a little girl.

-when had it happened?

dance asks himself as he watches his family climb the path toward him. soon they would be grown-folk. he realizes they are growing up right in front of his eyes and he was missing it. in the creeping shadows dance's keen eyes focus so hard on the children he has not yet noticed the wrinkled and slowly drying time. his son is the first to see his solitary figure rocking in the twilight and immediately starts to run toward dance, shouting,

-silence come thru the water! silence come
thru the water again!

time looks up when she hears her son shout. she watches as passage runs to his father and throws his arms around his neck. the two stand face to face in the growing darkness as passage tells his father all about the day's events. they are near reflections of one another. it is only then dance realizes that silence is barefooted, carrying her shoes in her hands. she smiles at dance as she passes him and continues up the porch and into the house.

tired, time stops near the large stump and stands there staring at the house, the sky, passage and his father. time can go no further. she wanted to get out of her wet clothes but time simply could not go another step. the simple refusal,

-no...

gently escapes from her lips so quietly she almost doesn't hear it. time didn't know how much more of this she could take.

-have you lost your wits?

the thought crosses her mind,

-if you still have a mind to cross, girl... guess they ain't lost yet.

time laughs in spite of herself. it starts out as just a little chuckle way down in the well of her stomach which for some reason by the time it reaches her mouth has become a scream. time stands there by the stump of the great tree and screams for her life.

passage and dance fall silent as their heads jerk in the direction of time. neither moves as they peer into the encroaching darkness at the stricken figure. silence hears her mother's scream and runs to the front door. she stands and looks through the screen. she feels the river angel in her hands pull toward time. led by the small blue angel silence walks slowly toward the screaming time and stands directly in front of her. silence holds out her arms to her mother and wraps them around her. in doing so the blue rock angel touches time's shoulder. the first thing time notices is the rock seems as warm as silence's flesh and nearly as soft, next this feeling of well being spreads from her shoulder, bathing her entire being. just as suddenly time stops screaming and hugs her child back.

dance crosses and within the ensuing silence time is gathered up into his arms and put to bed. silence prepares a simple dinner from the leftover chicken and rice she finds. when she and passage retire that night dance is sitting on the edge of the bed as time sleeps. for the first time in a very long time they find him there in the morning.

✳

thirty six

in the path of dance

-**w**hat you mean you pregnant?

-pregnant...

-as in goin' to have a baby? you? lord, lord!!! how gone
are you?

-nearly three months...

rita throws her head back and hollers. she laughs hard and
long. it is a bitter sweet laugh as once again she found it
hard to accept that she had been passed over for her friend.

-whose is it anyway?

melva jean throws rita a look and rolls her eyes.

-bitch!

-have you thought about what that woman gonna
do when she find out?

-ain't thought of nothin' else for the last week and a half.

-she a witch woman, you know that...

jealousy takes all forms. the image of naked dance came back and rita couldn't help herself. despite the stabbing pain she felt as she realized her unworthy friend was now carrying his child, she is still enjoying this way more than she should.

-have you told dance yet?

melva jean just shakes her head staring straight ahead, fighting a losing battle against tears standing at the ready.

-lord, what i'd give to be a fly on the wall when she find out...

-what am i gonna do?

melva jean asks to no one in particular, as she has everyday since the rabbit died.

-that is the very question i was gonna ask you myself.

rita starts to laugh again. she fights to control it. she catches the majority of it but there is still just a little that manages to escape from the sides of her grin.

-so sorry, couldn't help myself.

rita shakes off the rest.

-but really girl, what are you gonna do?

melva jean sits silently. suddenly the meaning of that silence hits rita. incredulously she asks,

-you not thinkin' of keepin' it? ...is you done lost yo' mind?

-ain't goin' to that crazy woman out in no woods near solace.

melva jean just shakes her head slightly and continues to stare straight ahead, unmindful of the two advancing tears clearing the mounds of her cheeks and running freely down the slope of her chin. rita is impressed in spite of herself,

-you know the bitch always been stuck up. well, well, well!!! this should bring her down a peg or two.

melva jean says nothing.

-a little dance...

rita continues. she touches melva jean's trembling arm.

-you scared?

-what you think? you say yourself she a witch woman. that bitch liable to kill me... or one of her aunts.

-should of thought of that before you opened your...

the look that melva jean shoots rita is enough to stop her mouth.

-bitch!,

cries melva jean as she stands up and slaps rita square across her face,

-don't care if i is pregnant, if you don't get the fuck out of my face i'm gonna kick your skinny black ass all the way back into them woods! heifer!

melva jean slammed the door but not hard enough she couldn't hear rita's shrill laughter as she sauntered down the road in pursuit of the first victim she could unload her dirty news onto. as it turns out rita runs into no one all the way to the roadhouse shanty, it being the feeding hour where everyone out all day had returned home and those out for the night had not yet left.

when she reaches the roadhouse rita is disappointed once again. there is only earl, who runs the place with his brother stuart and their grandfather william whom everybody calls daddy. earl entertains no conversation about anyone's private business. if the conversation is about anything other than what you are drinking or something as inane as the weather he would simply turn and walk away. rita surveys the one room looking for some shadow which could hide a potential listener but her search only uncovers the bookends as they are called, stanley and grover. in the roadhouse shanty they are fixtures. stanley is the oldest running customer having not missed a day in attendance in anyone's memory and grover is like old faithful. he is at the front door at opening and usually there when the lights cut off at night. they each have their usual corner and other than the controlled,

-another,

from grover or the clockwork raising of the right hand of stanley's every forty-five minutes or so indicating his need for a

-new glass of port,

they are silent. there is and has only ever been moonshine, that is what earl serves. other than these few syllables they are rarely heard from and seem most of the time to all but disappear into the woodwork in either corner, hence their nickname,

-the bookends.

this again is unsatisfactory for rita's retelling so she has to be content with squeezing what small amount of poisoned joy she could get out of replaying all the delicious details over in her little mind so as to not face the fact that melva jean possessed the one thing she, rita, had wanted since first laying eyes on dance and now proof of it too, his baby!

truly life is not fair, for if it were the seed dance planted nearly three months ago would not have taken root. dance had returned to sleeping at home over this last month, if not to time's bed at least to their bedroom. a certain peace seems to have settled around the house and no one could have been happier than passage to have dance at home for breakfast. so it is with a certain trepidation that dance received the note written by melva jean which she hand delivered to the quarry that afternoon. she arrived around lunch time and walked up to him, put the note in his hand, turned around and walked away. it was a simply written note,

-meet me at the roadhouse directly after work, it's
important!

it is because the important was underlined that dance decided to see her. he planned to call it off anyway, melva jean just didn't make him happy.

although it is true that life is not fair it is also true that every dog has its' day and so when dance walks into the bar early, bitch rita sits waiting to spring. she smiles to herself thinking,

-sometimes god is too good!

rita savors the moment. she doesn't want to rush it, it is too delicious to be gone too soon. she sits and waits as she watches dance come in and find his usual table near the backdoor. from there he could watch the comings and goings of the entire place and it afforded him a quick exit if ever needed. she lingers until he orders his first shot of shine as he settles in to wait for melva jean. she stays seated until after the second shot is brought to his table before she deliberately gets up and saunters over to the newly installed juke box. she deliberately chooses a song and inserts a nickel before she continues on to his table. she carries her glass of shine in one hand and holds the hand of the devil in the other.

-hello dance.

dance looks up from his drink and acknowledges rita's presence with a nod.

-haven't seen you in a while. where you been
keepin' yourself?

dance raises his shoulders in a noncommittal shrug.

-hear you back up the hill.

dance raises an eyebrow in response to rita's statement, definitely not used to discussing his comings and goings with her. it is here that rita's memory betrays her for then she remembers dance lying naked in melva jean's bed and found her mouth suddenly dry and herself feeling flush.

-damn, dance. you look good enough to eat!

rita put her hands on her hips to better accentuate the fine shape that was his to claim. dance just raises both eyebrows and lowers his head slightly as if to say,

-haven't we been through all this before.

-wanted the next dance... but guess it's already reserved,

rita's voice trails off as she lets her full meaning settle in,

-huh daddy?

she hisses, as she turns to see melva jean coming through the door. the look of confusion that crossed both faces at the same time is almost more than rita can stand and she breaks out into a vicious laugh as, without looking back at dance, she sashays past melva jean and out the front door.

※

thirty seven

in the path of dance

walking home through the woods that night dance has the distinct feeling that he is not alone. on the periphery of his vision he feels a familiar presence. if he had not been so troubled of heart and had not drunk three pitchers he would have paid more attention. melva jean's news threw him for a loop. he met with her with the intention of breaking it off. after all it wasn't working, he was sure they could both feel that. melva jean was a fine woman, just not his. as dance walked he could think of nothing but time, passage and silence. he couldn't help but think that he,

             –should have thought of them earlier...

he had been home these last six weeks and although he and time still have a distance to go, they were beginning to enjoy each other's company, they had even begun to laugh again. dance remembers how he felt when he first found out time was pregnant, the anticipation, the racing heart and the boundless joy. he compares that to this feeling of despair, confusion and alienation he was now experiencing. dance would have to tell time, tonight, before rita's mouth could bring it to her ears, if it hadn't already. time is a proud woman. he knows she is not going to take this well.

-what woman would?

he asks himself. all her past transgressions would pale in comparison to this. dance has learned this much about women, although she might be able to overlook his sleeping with melva jean she never would a child. dance is standing at the crossroads near the edge of the woods where he had first seen time. so lost in thought is he that he actually passes the dark sitting figure before she speaks,

-so boy, now you gonna walk on and not say anything? know done raised you better than that...

dance freezes. he could feel the hair on the back of his neck rise up. he spins around to find the dancing eyes of miss margaret sitting on a large rock, on her lap her familiar large black and gold cat which she pets unconsciously. dance would have been scared but at the seat of his soul he knew no matter what form she took, miss margaret would never do him any harm.

-ain't you got nothin' to say? come sit a spell and talk with an old 'oman.

miss margaret's eyes glint in the light of the rising moon.

-what's wrong? cat got your tongue?

although she never smiled, dance could always tell when

miss margaret was enjoying herself. this was one of those times. he could smell the scent of rosemary associated with her presence. there was no sign her spirit had gone through fire. dance is just about to reach out to hug her when miss margaret admonishes him with,

-don't touch me boy, less'n you ready to come back
with me tonight and child it ain't yo' time.

dance stop. can't stay long, so be still and listen.

dance, ever the obedient son, sits down in the center of the crossroad and waits. after a spell, miss margaret keeping her eyes fixed on him, slowly lowers her head and gives him a look, then she turns her head and spits. dance feels as he had as a child when about to get reprimanded.

-what's done's done. there ain't nothin' to do about
yesterday... the trials are upon you. don't forget all that i
done study you. listen to the wind, child. follow her
council and respect the old ways. i will be waitin' for you
at the bottom of the well.

miss margaret puts the cat down and slowly rises to her feet,

-you can't sleep again in that house.
this time, she will kill you.

the ancient figure turns to go and begins to walk off. she stops and without turning around offers,

-look to your first born son. he need you...

she is almost lost into the darkness of the woods when she turns and for the first time that dance could remember miss margaret smiled,

-i will not pass your way again.

she was already returning into the arms of eternity when he heard her voice one last time,

-tell silence to reach for the eye of the storm...

and then she was gone.

❋

thirty eight

in the path of time

-**if** you lays down with dogs you surely gets up with fleas,

aunt affection offers freely to the universe and to no one in particular at the same time. she studies the long setting sun and remembers that this is the day of the summer solstice. baby girl had not said a word for the last hour or so since she and then aunt cinnamon arrived. time looks without seeing and watches with no cognition.

bernice came over to time as soon as rita left her house. she had not even waited for the reverend to finish his supper. bernice wanted time to hear about it as soon as possible. although she dreaded telling her, bernice knew it would hurt so much more if it was something picked up in the streets or if she knew bernice had known and not told her. bernice is sure rita would take every opportunity to drop this news wherever she traveled like a horse after too many apples.

-lyn and i just about to sit down to supper when there's this knock on the door. time, you could have floored me when i looks up and there stands rita. now you know in all the years been livin' here rita johnston ain't never darkened my doorway, so i's thinkin' she must be here to see lyn. figure somebody died or some such, though she wasn't really dressed for death. well, to each his own...

it isn't that bernice was trying to draw it out, she just couldn't bare to hurt her friend. time sits patiently and waits for bernice to go on. this is uncharacteristic of bernice to ramble on so and she also knows it is rare for bernice to carry something. time knows it must be really important.

-invited her in but god forgive me just couldn't bring
          myself to offer her some of my supper.

     -most folks might have excused theyselves until after
               you finished eatin',

comments time.

     -want to make some arrangements, rita begins, for
          christenin'... goin' to be a godmother.

-'member thinkin' hadn't heard of anyone givin' birth here lately but didn't say anythin'. got the book to write down the details. when i ask her the name of the parents...

here again bernice hesitates,

     -she say melva jean patterson and... dance.

time says nothing and continues sewing the edges of the multicolored square she planned to use in a new quilt. she put down the basket and looks up to see the dying colors of the sun which is about to set. time knew dance had been down at melva jean's since he left her bed but this was somehow different. there is a permanence in a child and a certain disrespect. bernice was worried. there are any manner of edicts regarding scorned women all leading to death and destruction. she would feel better if time cried or ranted and raved but this continued silence, sitting there in the growing dark watching fireflies, scared her. as dusk arrives so does aunt affection and soon after that aunt cinnamon. having gotten a whiff of rita's droppings they came to support their niece. bernice stands to leave as soon as she sees them enter the yard. time stands up and hugs her friend tightly. she has nothing to say but she wants bernice to know how much she appreciated what she had done.

-evenin' miss affection, miss cinnamon,

bernice calls out as she passes the two elders in the yard.

-how's baby girl?

asks aunt affection. bernice just shakes her head. aunt cinnamon sucks her teeth and continues on her bad feet to the porch where she pats her niece on her shoulder and into the house to find her grand-niece and nephew. aunt affection comes on up on the porch and sits down. she takes one good look at time and for the first time that anyone could remember aunt affection was at a loss for words. time just sat and rocked. she stared out from eyes hard as stone seeing nothing of the view from the porch and tasting only the bitter nectar of rage which proceeded the blaze of revenge sure to follow. time sits there and gathers her spirit, preparing herself. she will need the added strength and clarity of focus in this upcoming battle which has fallen upon her. time can't breathe as if she is drowning. she is fighting for air, for her life, for its' very meaning and purpose. time knows she is a strong woman but it isn't until,

-dance's bastard,

all time would ever call the child, enters her world that she knows how powerful. it is a blessing that time lacked true knowledge of her strength for if she had conscious control of her power she would have had no restraint. the magnitude of her pain was unparalleled and her hatred knew no bounds. for the first time she discovers dark, dank places deep in the far recesses of her soul, the depths of which she's never imagined. unconsciously from within the very core of her being a cry rings out with such anguish it touches the white haired thicket-women who stand on the shores of the sacred sea across the waters from sanctuary. time reaches inside and unknowingly calls to these ancient women who guard her line. hearing their daughter's cry in the great wilderness they respond and in turn begin to sing loudly enough for time to hear and be soothed by their song. their

221

melody carries her to resolution. by the time that dance appears around the bend in the road time had gathered all of his belongings outside the door of the outhouse. she has time to leisurely empty all of his clothes, shoes and tools into the hole before turning her back and strolling away.

-shit to shit!

there was nothing of his that dance could take. when he leaves the outhouse dance crosses the yard and steps onto the porch. the front door for the first time that anyone could remember was locked. passage watches from the window above as dance stands there on the front porch and stares at the outhouse that now held all of his possessions. he stands there for a minute or so trying to regain balance, trying to remember when things got this wrong. he realizes that again he only has the clothes on his back and that he is lucky he was wearing his work boots, they would have been the hardest to replace.

passage makes a decision and hurriedly gathers what few of his possessions he could carry so he would not be left behind. from the doorway silence watches passage and even without seeing out of the window knows what is occurring. as passage turns to leave his eyes meet his sister's. the real possibility of being away from each other for the first time crosses their mind at the same time. there is no need for words, they understand each other and read each others thoughts as they have since birth. silence finds she suddenly can't go downstairs. she can't say goodbye, not to passage. silence goes and gets her river angel and sits on the top step and fights back tears she feels gathering.

time watches passage come down carrying his pillowcase filled with clothes and still it takes her a little while before she realizes what is happening. it is only as he reaches the back door she understands that passage intends to leave.

-and just where you think you're goin'?

passage stands still and says nothing. his silence seems to infuriate time even more. she doesn't even notice the high pitched shrill that enters her voice as she shouts to passage,

-don't you hear me talkin' to you, young man, just where you think you're goin'?

passage turns to his mother and for the first time she sees in his eyes the man he has become. for a second time is able to grasp the damage done to passage during the bitterness and bile of the separation between herself and dance. passage stands his ground and looking very much like his father's son gives her a look so filled with hatred that it chills her heart. very quietly, with a conviction that is not to be questioned he answers simply,

-with my father.

dance is about to turn and go, he has no idea where when he hears the commotion in the house. he heard time's voice raised though he couldn't quite make out what was being said. suddenly he hears the back door slam and footsteps running around the side of the house. passage tosses down the pillowcase full of hastily gathered possessions, runs up to his father and throws his arms around dance's chest.

-don't go, less'n you take me with you. won't stay
here if you leave.

dance looks down into the earnest eyes of passage and hears miss margaret's instructions,

-look to your first born son. he need you,

and indeed it was passage standing before him, tugging at his clothing. there was no sign of his sister. silence watches dance and passage walk away until well after the sunset on the longest day of the year, yet only passage knows how long silence stood staring out of that window, alone.

✳

thirty nine

in the path of dance

they truly have no idea, father and son, where they are headed for as they walk down the path away from their home they do so unconsciously. dance spots time's aunts coming down the road, drawn by his departure no doubt and as he is in no state of mind to deal with them now he turns toward the woods. dance tries to get depressed for a moment for once again he has lost everything but then he had only to look to his left at the bouncing shadow of passage to know that this was not entirely true. this time he had his son and with that treasure he would never again be without.

-what you cryin' for boy?

dance hears clearly in miss margaret's voice,

-endin's are always just new beginnin's...

dance and passage walk for the better part of the night while dance thinks which he does best while walking. suddenly given to a memory from the farm, dance begins telling his son a story from his childhood. dance seldom thinks of massa's farm and remembrances from those days appear rarely. dance could see himself and a number of other children around a fire, he remembers that entire day. it must have been the fourth of july, the only day massa gave slaves the whole day off. in summer they even worked a half-day on sundays. he ate good on that day, fried chicken, potato salad and cornbread their holiday feast. at night time they broke open watermelons that had cooled all day in the stream. all the children sat around this fire while old ben-j'min told the story of these three brothers,

> -shada-rack, me-shack and a-bend-day-go... who come
> through the fire... but they never get boynt...

dance could still hear old benj'min's voice. dance had been mesmerized by the story thinking what it must feel like to not be burned by fire.

> -kinda like the opposite of silence comin' thru the
> water and not gettin' drownt.

dance breaks into a laugh as he looks at his son with a new appreciation.

> -like shada-rack, me-shack and a-bend-day-go...

sings out dance and passage follows suit. soon the solstice moon is high in the serene blue stillness. that sky once again epitomized the embodiment of freedom and its' promise of expectation. perhaps even passage catches a glimpse of god's perfection. by the time the moon reaches its' zenith, high in the cloudless heavens, dance had a plan. a calmness seemed to descend as that night they slept under the stars.

blue river comes upon father and son the next day as they sit by the bank of the brook. he's been out all morning checking his traps and blue river found so many fish that he is having a hard time carrying home his catch.

-mornin' mr. blue,

greets passage as he jumps up to help blue river with the two baskets over brimming.

-well good mornin' to you, passage and i thanks for helpin' to make an old man's burdens lighter. dance.

-blue. got quite a haul there.

-don't know what it is. fish seem like they just jumping into the traps like they wants to be caught. they still two traps ain't had time to check yet... it's a good boy you got there,

blue river observes as he realizes that passage has taken both baskets and is moving them into the fast diminishing shade.

-come and help me eat some of this fish, there ain't but so much one can dry or carry or clean.

it is something in the way blue river speaks as he studies the pounds of fish that strikes them both funny and their chuckle grows into a howl. passage looks up and smiles from across the clearing at his father laughing with his friend. passage feels himself in the world of men. father and son would grow to know each other and passage would account this summer as the happiest in his life.

with the help of blue river and the two washington brothers by the first week in august dance had built a two room cabin. technically on blue river's land, it borders the land left to time. it's so good for passage to be out working in the sun, he is just at the age where muscles and skeletal frame channel the first strong push of hormones. passage was growing like a weed, his chest and his feet most notably. he ate everything in sight and literally seemed to get bigger each time he slept.

working around the washington brothers broadened passage's horizons in other ways as well, especially from bob washington who always had tidbits to,

-pass on,

as he would explain to passage,

-the ways of life.

passage gained a perspective and insight into the mysterious world of women. it is here through innuendo that he first encounters such mysteries as,

> -gettin' head, the joys of findin' a snapper or the woes
> of comin down with the clap.

it is here that passage first hears melva jean's name in relationship to his father, her pregnancy and of the baby coming that belongs to dance.

> -seent melva jean the other day,

roy washington begins. they had just finished laying the foundation and were sitting down to a lunch fannie elizabeth fixed for their repast before beginning to put up the walls. it was an exceptionally good meal consisting of deviled eggs, fried chicken sandwiches, lemonade and a wedge of her double lemon pound cake for each of them. the truth is that fannie elizabeth was secretly elated with the breakup of time's happy home and saw her lunches as a way of supplying the troops helping consolidate the toppling of

> -miss time off her high and mighty throne!

so fannie elizabeth took it on as a sacred duty, besides she had to feed her two men to keep up their strength.

> -she definitely beginnin' to show,

roy washington continued,

-what i wants to know is can you be sure the baby yourn?

bob washington asks, oblivious to the irony that his posing
this question represents, after all his or roy's seventh child,
buster having been born only two months earlier.

passage stops chewing and dance feels the eyes of his son on
his back. he turns to face passage. dance is not one to keep
truth from his boy and living together as men, he sees little
reason to shelter him now. passage looks at his father with
new eyes and dance observes the difference in them. it now
all makes sense, the fighting, the shouting and the violence.
this is a dance passage does not know. it has been liberating
living free with dance. this summer, living outside, dance
seemed to come to life in a different way. passage learned
how much his father knew about survival in the woods,
about which plants were edible and which plants heal.
passage learned about cloud shifting and how to smell upcoming rain. he learned how to build a lean-to or a fire,
swing a hammock, about the green language and he learned
about melva jean.

-it's tru'. you got any questions for me?

passage doesn't know exactly how to feel. on the one hand
he feels his mother's betrayal but then on the other hand he
knows what it's been like to live with time. either way, this

was between them. passage shakes his head and though he never looks at dance quite the same, he asks him nothing. when he looked back passage would remember what he learned about most of all that summer was the ferocity of his father's laughter, that dance was only a man and judging by the frequency of his own erections apparently so too now was he.

✳

forty

in the path of silence

it is silence who is most affected, for when dance leaves he takes with him passage. this is the first time that the siblings have ever been apart this long and silence feels their separation profoundly. since the onset of her menstrual flow three years earlier there has been some distancing between brother and sister yet they were rarely far away from each other's thoughts. it had been mostly silence who found it comfortable to shield some of her woman thoughts from her brother but the connection had been constant, now there was interference. sometimes the image was there, crystal clear, strong as it had always been then sometimes a dull aching nothing. in this void silence felt alone. she has never had friends. between her iridescent skin and reappearances, sustained contacts with other children had been few and far between. although towns-folk caution their children to always,

-be very nice to...

no one ever allowed their child to play with or even get too close to silence, for fear that she might disappear with their child in tow. in school she sat alone. passage had been her only refuge and now with him gone and time retired, except for the solitary visits of her grand-aunts silence is unaccompanied. on her own she quickly adjusts. during the day silence takes to wandering. silence would get up early, clean the house from head to toe, in case a grand-aunt dropped by and then leave. silence finds if she is lucky she could get all her chores done, dinner cooked and be out the door by ten-thirty or eleven, long as her grand-aunt affection hadn't caught her first.

-not a decent hour for a young girl to be gallivantin' if
she ain't got no place in particular to be.

if grand-aunt cinnamon was anywhere within earshot she would come to her rescue. under her breath she would comment,

-some folks aught to keep they lips out of other
folks' business,

then she would let a few minutes go by before saying innocently,

-these flowers need changin'. silence, would you be a
darlin' and go pick me a bunch of your mother's
wildflowers for the dinin' room table?

sending time out under the glare of aunt affection who never contradicted her sister.

for company silence begins to rely on her river angel and she takes him everywhere. it is on one of these morning outings that silence, following a wildflower trail, discovers the tiny graveyard. wildflowers grow all over, encircling it entirely. silence recognizes her mother's touch. she feels drawn to the one simple grave and comes there almost every day. after visiting the lone grave, silence sets out in a different direction and each day would eventually find herself being led by her river angel down to the waters near blue river's cabin. silence spent hours sitting dangling her feet down into the edge of the cool brook waters, talking with her angel for silence found that the river angel spoke into her thoughts and her river angel would tell her things.

one day she heard this moan float on the wind and the more she listened it sounded like a tune. silence had to sit perfectly still so as not to miss the slightest note. it seems the voices came from across the brook near blue river's cabin. more than once she had been tempted to cross the waters in search of their origin. then before her eyes she saw perfectly clear the white sands of a beach and this thicket under purple skies with two golden moons and it all looked so familiar. growing alongside the waters' edge were bushes of old woman singing ceaseless tunes both beautiful and haunting. another day she saw a bridge of fire and a sky of lightning, not accompanied by the usual thunder. for some reason the concept of silent lightning intrigued silence. on several other occasions silence would catch a hint of their song, ever so faintly.

in her sojourns silence loved to observe folks. it's amazing how when you don't speak people assume you can't hear and will say almost anything in front of you. in her travels silence ran into evil in the forms of miss rita and miss fannie elizabeth. miss rita said the most peculiar thing.

-ooo lord chile, better hope this baby of melva jean's ain't
no 'bino. it sure do run through a family.

strangest thing is they were both still looking directly at silence when miss fannie elizabeth added,

-and i hope the chile not dumb, like its' sista.

they laugh a vicious laugh.

-and they better pray it look like dance.

adds miss rita.

-if indeed he even the daddy,

concludes miss fannie elizabeth as they both stroll off laughing, their amble backsides jiggling behind them. watching the two women walking away silence wishes passage nearby to share thoughts with for in this way silence too finds out about dance's upcoming arrival.

✳

forty one

in the path of cinnamon

aunt affection's death comes as quite a shock to everyone
and although she never sheds a public tear, no one is more
affected than aunt cinnamon.

   -just like her... so much left undone, unsaid, unfinished,

aunt cinnamon thinks as she stands over her sister's maple-
wood casket in the little church. she knows this is the way
of death but it is also so much like affection too. cinnamon
was sure affection,

       -just didn't want to think of dyin'...

didn't leave a will, not a piece of paper, no instructions,
nothing. left cinnamon and baby girl to sort everything out.

affection's funeral had been surreal for cinnamon. the
strangest thing of all actually occurred the night of her death
when cinnamon, usually a very sound sleeper suddenly
awakened calling affection's name. it sounded strange
because true to her word, cinnamon had not spoken her sister's name in the five years since that hateful anointing in
the kitchen. cinnamon had been dreaming and in the

dream she and her sister couldn't have been more than five or six playing outside the back door of their massa's house. there had been an auction on the farm that day since which she had not been able to find her sister, she'd looked everywhere. at just that moment in the dream cinnamon realizes affection has been sold and is frantically calling her name when cinnamon awakens, tears streaming down her face. the dream seemed too eerily real. cinnamon had not visited the slave farm in her dreams for years.

cinnamon realized that her vow's been involuntarily broken but had no idea the full ramifications of her vision or she might have hurried to her sister's side. even for the five years they didn't speak they still lived in the same house and were silent company for each other. cinnamon didn't get up that night and was haunted by that fact for years. she realized afterwards that this dream occurred probably at about the same time affection was passing and if she had just come into the room that night cinnamon might have heard affection apologize before her demise.

affection had been a proud woman and always thought of herself as a gentle christian. the burden of that release of spittle those five years ago and the chasm it created proved more than affection could bear. the horror she glimpsed in herself and the knowledge of the depth of hatred she had been able to provoke in her sister was far more than affection could admit to. eventually its' weight wore her down and scared her even now as with apprehension she made her way down the corridor towards the light of her creator. it was the only thing on her ledger for which she had no excuse. she wanted to apologize, had always meant to, well as soon as the passion of the moment died down but she just couldn't find the way. it somehow seemed so hard and the words never would come until now when it was too late.

righteous cinnamon made her task no easier. the look of pure hatred cinnamon shot her that afternoon from the floor, coupled with the fact that cinnamon seemed well able to continue on happily with her life, without anymore apparent thought to affection, only made matters worse. for cinnamon, affection no longer seemed to exist. the more time passed the greater the distance became, especially when the look of resigned hatred turned to cold indifference. so when death's icy fist grabbed hold of her that last night affection was unprepared. the one cry of regret affection uttered before her time finished and she taken to glory was,

-oh please lord, not yet, i still have to tell the heifer
i's sorry...

and so the last thought affection had in this life was of her sister cinnamon's apology.

the strangest thing about affection's passing was the enormity of the eldership which quietly fell to cinnamon. with it came unexpected responsibilities she never imagined. the gifts everyone always assumed were affection's alone with her death passed onto her surviving sister. it was aunt cinnamon who seemed to now have the gift of sight, a gift she had never noticed before until her sister's passing. it was almost as if affection transferred her magic to her sister. cinnamon's healing light had always been hidden behind affection's. now it was aunt cinnamon whom the young women sought out when time to deliver or when newlyweds who were fighting didn't feel to take it to the new pastor. the dispensing of wisdom, something aunt cinnamon rarely gave out before, was now expected. there seemed no end to the constant stream of women in need of this or that and as hard as she would have been pressed to admit it, old crusty aunt cinnamon relished this sense of being needed. she enjoyed the inheritance of being the village elder. it almost made up for the loneliness that the absence of affection left. unfortunately nothing made up for the fact that non-apologizing affection died alone in the next room and that she, cinnamon, her only surviving sister, had not been by her side, brought her a glass of water or even gotten up to say goodbye.

✳

forty two

in the path of time

it isn't only passage and dance's absence affecting silence so, there is also a change palatable in the house and evident in time. what great joy time once held inside was not only suddenly dried up but replaced by something vile, like the affect of slow acting cancer creeping up on an unsuspecting victim, often time never claiming the very individual it is in the process of taking until deaths' final grasp. dying could be so quiet and took so many forms. with both dance and passage gone and only the occasional shadow of silence, time retreats to her room. she even refuses to see her aunt. as is her way, time takes to sleeping, seeking solace in her dreams. at first she makes appearances a couple of times a day for meals but soon even that proves to be too great a struggle. next she begins taking her meals in her room, served on a tray by silence for which she awakens and sits up in bed to receive. that is her only contact with her daughter and the conscious world outside. by the time that the leaves begin to turn time sleeps almost all of the time. although the doctor is called in repeatedly there seems to be nothing wrong and nothing he can do. time simply refuses to get out of bed and prefers sleeping to all other forms of stimulation. time's dream world is truly engulfing and she willingly surrenders to its' lure. by the harvest moon she is sleeping away most of the day but when time declines to come to table thanksgiving day aunt cinnamon finally has had enough,

-well i'll be god-damned!

a silence falls over the table for no one had ever heard aunt cinnamon call out the lord's name like she did after leaving time's yawning refusal to come and sit with the family before turning her back on her aunt and pulling the covers over her head.

-all the heifer got to do is come and sit down at the god-damned table! shit it ain't like her rusty butt helped cook a thing.

aunt cinnamon shouted loud enough she was sure time could hear,

-should feel lucky someone think enough to bring thanks-givin' over to her trifling behind. lord if this don't beat all. this take the cake! the whole entire cake, frostin' and everythin'! and over some man, a god-damned man! lord never thought i'd live to see the day. so glad her mama dead and in her grave so she don't have to look on no mess like this, cause that 'zactly what we have here, a mess. as god is my witness, a pure-d mess!

and with that aunt cinnamon sits down, folds her hands, bows her head and asks blue river to,

–please bless the table!

✳

forty three

in the path of time

the closer it gets to the birth of,

-dance's bastard,

the more time sleeps. she finds power hidden in her dreams. studying sleep like a free diver, she reaches for greater depths with every swim and in her dream state time realizes consciousness. within her astral body time creates thought forms which manifest in the awakened world around her. while asleep time is able to project herself and her will. here in this dark terrain of the dream world time is let free to run wild and like a cub testing its' claws, strikes out. in her present rage she discovers her savagery knows no bounds. time is way under in a deep self-induced coma. she realized suddenly that at this depth the automated functions operated without any attention needed and freed her to work more efficiently. her target was dance's bastard but time had to first weigh down the dreams of sanctuary.

to the awakened world time seemed an invalid but when she slept time's sublimated rage made for dreams that were not only powerful but disturbing everyone! at first no one noticed, it was just that no one could get a goodnight's sleep.

there just seemed to be,

-somethin' wrong...

-somethin' on my mind...

-somethin' with the old feather mattress...

-somethin' that didn't sit well on my stomach from last
nights' supper...

-somethin' wakin' me up in the middle of the night and
keepin' me from gettin' back to sleep...

-somethin' not right, just can't put my finger on it...

it is a violation, the visitation that befalls the little town the
day melva jean goes into labor. so as to make the town
oversleep time even sent the birds to doze so they would
not disturb the dawn. when the sun rises that morning blue
river is the first to notice the absence of the birds' song. for
blue river, alone, way out in the woods, the silence is thun-
derous. aunt cinnamon is the next to notice. she awakens
late and notices that the morning seems strangely devoid of
life. there are no morning sounds as the town slumbers.

time then turns her attentions to dance's bastard and her first
target, its' heifer of a mother. rather than sneak away to
some hidden corner of the world the brazen hussy parades

244

dance's seed in her pregnant body in front of time's face.

    -is the bitch crazy? she must don't know...

time clutches at the life within, breaking melva jean's water early. aunt cinnamon suddenly feels a strange chill and sits up alarmed. listening into the morning-less air she hears silence and then a muffled scream. reaching for her robe aunt cinnamon gets out of bed and instinctively begins to gather her birthing tools. she'd felt the imminent birth of every child in sanctuary since affection died. she gathers her satchel, salves and prepared herbs dried for this situation. without being told she knows melva jean has gone into premature labor. aunt cinnamon brews herself a large cup of black coffee, sweet, cuts herself a slice of onion bread she made the day before and sits down to wait for a knock on her door which never comes

from the onset of labor time hovers, biding her time as power awaits evil, those of insatiable hunger, willing to give all for momentary satisfaction. power understands there is no need to chase these fools for they inevitably find their way back to evil, further fueling the fires of their own extinction. unable to disturb the grace of the child time calls to death melva jean and feeds off of the misery her darkness disperses just as evil fed off of time.

it isn't until much later into the day that aunt cinnamon learns what happened. she had dozed off while her pot of vegetable soup settled and was awakened by the sound of an automobile pulling up to the house. she is surprised to see rita emerge. aunt cinnamon almost doesn't recognize her. rita has on no make-up and looked like she had been up all night crying.

-miss cinnamon, so sorry to disturb.

-that's all right rita girl, come on in. like somethin' to eat?
got a nice piece a blackberry cobbler in the cooler
from last night's supper in there. you want i cut you
a little piece?

-no thank you, miss cinnamon, can't stay… melva jean
died this mornin' on the way to the hospital.

-in salvation?

-yes ma'am. baby came quick and she delivered in the
back seat. all of a sudden she just starts bleedin'…

rita begins to cry, softly,

-there was so much blood. she just held her baby and
smiled this little smile. by the time we got to the
hospital she was already gone.

aunt cinnamon takes rita into her arms, rita cries in earnest.

-the child?

-it's a boy.

-where he at?

-in the backseat of the car.

aunt cinnamon looks at rita like she crazy as the elderly woman moves towards the front door.

-you got the baby here, now? jesus lord have mercy, you left the baby out in the car? i do declare rita johnston you ain't got the good sense the lord done give you. go get that child and bring it in the house!

-i din't know where else to bring him, melva jean don't have no kin.

-and he ain't no kin to me... he all right?

aunt cinnamon asks as rita lifts the child from the back seat. rita nods her head, then says sadly,

-look just like dance.

✳

forty four

in the path of dance

-most thick enough to cut. idn't it?

-ma'am?

asks dance who has just run into miss cinnamon standing
waiting for him at the crossroads. dance always liked her.
there was something in her gruffness he found familiar. she
was direct. in some ways she reminded him of miss margaret. miss cinnamon always impressed him as someone fair.
in all the months he and time have been apart she's never
asked him any questions, never treated him any different. it
was none of her business and she stayed out of his affairs.
now this here was different...

-the air around here seem kind of heavy.

-yes ma'am, it surely do.

remarks dance as he looks around at the fog that had settled
in. this is the second day the sun had vacated in deference
to this density and even though his time piece reads nearly
eleven, there was no sign to distinguish morning.

-you ever seen fog like this before?

-no ma'am.

-well neither has i and i's pass eighty-some-odd-year.

aunt cinnamon studies dance for a moment and takes in a
slow inhalation.

-son, been waitin' on you. has some bad news.

never one to prolong, she states,

-melva jean give birth to a man-child yesterday mornin'.
on her way to the hospital over there in salvation… they
was complications. the baby's fine…

aunt cinnamon takes a breath. before dance can ask she adds
simply,

-melva jean dead. …she didn't make it.

it takes dance a moment to take it all in.

-melva jean dead? how? baby waren't due for
another six weeks.

this is something dance had never considered.

-he's here now and the question be what you
gonna do with him?

-what i gonna do?

dance repeats, still dazed by the speed in which circumstances change.

-you's the daddy ain't you? well he layin' up with no
name. first thing you got to do be go claim yo' child.

dance loved few things in this life, dance feared to love.
what he loved always managed to be taken from him. he
loved freedom and she was suddenly gone one night, forced
by the rape to leave. he loved miss margaret and she was
gone in one moment, lost to that morning fire and then
there was time, whom he had loved the most, lost to a
paralyzing sleep and most assuredly melva jean now was
forever lost to dance. passage and silence were the only
evidence of his having existed on the earth, until now and
even that joy was diminished within his growing suspicion
that silence wasn't his and truthfully this child melva jean
dropped could rightfully belong to... dance had to stop.
there are adages regarding speaking ill of the dead and dance
never heard talk of melva jean with anyone else after he
took up with her. dance remembered the size of his erec-

tion that morning rita discovered them and he needed no
genius to do the math... this baby belonged to him.

-where the child at?

-over there at rita's.

-at rita's! miss cinnamon?...

-drivin' her crazy. rita was drivin' the roadster when
melva jean give birth. afterwards there waren't no need
to linger on in salvation... so she took melva jean on
up to mr. doke's. melva jean all alone in the world.
didn't have no family. naturally rita took the baby
home with her.

lord, they saying that baby givin' rita fits. say it won't
take no bottle. lost angel screamin' his little head off, god
bless his soul... like to bring the heavens down. poor little
thing. it's hard to lose your mama at birth, hard to make it
in this world and they say rita's takin' it right poorly too,
havin' been there... and after all she and melva jean
was best friends.

dance has already turned in the direction of town.

paths of sanctuary

-thank you miss cinnamon,

he threw over his shoulder as he stepped out. her work done, aunt cinnamon stands watching dance's long gaited stride as he distances himself down the road. dance had not disappointed. she comments to herself aloud,

-like that boy, always have. baby girl could have done
a lot worse for herself.... a lot worse.

from the moment he lays eyes on him dance knows it is his son. the baby looks just like passage had the first time he had seen him and both looked just like dance. crying like a motherless child since the death of melva jean, the moment dance touches his son the child quiets and makes only gurgling noises.

-well i'll be damned, that's the first time the little bastard
done shut up in two days,

complains rita as the baby falls asleep in dance's arms.

-god, there is a reason i ain't got no children...
take your baby, please and go!

and so dance carried his second son home.

＊

252

forty five

in the path of dance

rita cries quietly into her handkerchief as she sits on the second row for her best friend's home-going. the parishioners think they see the grief of one lost friend for another but what they really witness is rita's awakening. melva jean's death affects rita terribly. she becomes a changed soul. from the time of that aborted ride ending at the undertakers, rita has not taken a drink or sought out the company of her usual set. as she sat there now, all she could think about was her own passing and how empty the church would be. with melva jean dying and leaving her with the burial, rita realized just how much death cost. if she were to die today or tomorrow there would be no one to put her in the ground. the weight of that truth was almost more than she could bare

when dance enters the church carrying his son to its' mother's funeral he still has not named him. dance proceeds to the front seats which have been left for him and passage, who walks beside him. silence stayed home with sleeping time. dance feels peculiar in the seat reserved for family before realizing that he carries in his arms all of melva jean's family and even if the child is only four days old, it had a right to sit on the front row of mourners.

-the distance is never greater than when the goal is
closest and yet so many never finish the race... no, not in
our time but in god's time and in god's good grace.

dance, rita and the congregation look up to the pulpit. the
reverend falcon continues,

-i had the opportunity to speak with our dearly
departed sista just this pass sunday right here on the front
steps of the parsonage. she was so excited about the
upcomin' blessed event. man makes plans but only god
has the master plan. the rest of today is not promised to
anyone and tomorrow is but a mere twinkle in his glance.
the good lord saw fit to take our dear sista melva jean.
but god in his infinite wisdom left us her son to raise.

amen!

the bible says rejoice at our goin' out and sorrow at our
comin' in. if you have tears cry not for our sista recently
departed for her time of toil in this world of troubles has
come to an end. cry instead for this child whom god has
left to make his way in this world without a mother's love.
for sista melva jean the trials of this life are long over. let
us pray for the soul of our departed sista and for the gift
that the lord chose to leave us in her stead. let us pray
for we whom god has left behind.

reverend falcon then looked down directly at dance sitting

there holding one son on his lap and his other at his side. as if on cue the baby lets out a wail.

-and may we be diligent in our responsibilities to this little child as each and everyone of us here will be held accountable. the salvation of our very souls may depend on it. this motherless child who cries unto the wilderness now belongs to us all. with god's grace may we prove worthy to his blessin'. now let the congregation say amen.

it is then that dance hears clearly in miss margaret's voice,

-gotta give the baby a chance...

and there it was. dance would name his second son chance and pray for his tomorrow.

※

forty six

in the path of time

time had finally found her power. as with all great gifts it came with a high tariff for there is always a price to pay... if you don't use the gifts they in turn will use you. if you misuse the gifts they will surely misuse you. humility is often underrated for the blessing is never really yours, it only comes through you. you never own your talents and when you start to think you do that is when they truly own you. one must always recognize one's limits. unaware of the destruction she was causing to herself, time had not awakened in three days to take nourishment or even to relieve herself. silence goes in several times to check-see if time is still breathing. time gets high off the new found abilities she unconsciously discovers and uncaringly uses. without examining the question of soul nor the karmic issues of retribution, time is nearing the point of simply straining her physical body to death. time is literally wasting away as evil gluts its' fill.

often what you fear most you bring to yourself and so it was as time first hears dance's baby cry. in hating its' mother to death and in attempting to keep it away, time had brought dance's bastard to herself. dance decides it is time for chance to meet his brother and sister. dance still needs to figure out how to raise a newborn and keep his job at the quarry too. passage and silence cross to the gate when they see dance with their brother. they stand there for some time each holding the newborn, they start towards the house but as soon as chance gets within reach of time's inner circle of power he inexplicably lets out an explosive scream awakening time. he begins to wail and shriek in earnest. almost immediately the fog which hung over the village since the morning of his birth begins dissipating. when dance comes in to see time she is not ready to face him yet so she heads back for the cover and safety of sleep but each and every time she reaches its' border, chance's screams force time's return. apparently there is no way for time to hold onto power unless she is sleeping and there is no way to reach that level of sleep as the baby shrieks whenever his energy comes in contact with the force that stole his mother.

there was always some suspicion as to time's full participation in melva jean's death but it's difficult to convict someone for something occurring while they sleep or even blame someone for their dreams. there are a few people who put together the onset of labor and time's extended nocturnal. uncharacteristically dance is not among the suspicious for with a new born on his hands he finds his plate suddenly very full.

that next morning blue river hears birds again.

✳

forty seven

in the path of silence

-leave it to chance...

of the divine powers grace is the greatest and grace chose a man-child named chance to reside in. so it was for a time grace walked the earth and there was not a soul who came into contact who was not touched by his charm. he was a little boy beloved by everyone. for the baby chance there was an endless stream of booties and gowns, embroidered from ancient hands with best intentions that felt they just had to do,

-somethin' for the poor little motherless thing.

an angel due to circumstances of an unfortunate birth had been released, left to fend for itself. no matter what they may have thought of melva jean and dance or the way chance arrived, town-folks were naturally drawn to chance unlike any other child they had known. folks felt a compulsion to love this child for as the reverend pointed out he was theirs collectively. they joyously gave to chance of their bounty and in loving him so brought down many blessings upon themselves. all those who gave to chance brought in a bumper crop that year. there was no one he met who wasn't beguiled by his eyes or disarmed by his smile. even time found herself drawn to chance, despite herself. once dance came in to find time changing his diaper and singing to him,

> -well, you wouldn't expect me to let the baby just lay
> there wet, would you?

another time dance walked in to find her playing,

> -fingers and toes.

chance couldn't find a refuge against love anywhere in sanctuary except for maybe aunt cinnamon who did not believe in spoiling children.

> -they's rotten enough when they gets old enough to smell
> theyselves and so much worse if they gets spoilt first,

but truth was chance really only reveled at the shores and bathed in the light of blue river. even as a baby, whenever blue river entered a room it was as if the sun's arrival awakened the bloom of a tepid sky blossom. chance jumped up and screamed with his arms outstretched and could not be stilled until held securely within blue river's grasp. suddenly chance's screams turned into great peals of laughter. so it was only a natural progression for dance to ask blue river to watch chance while dance was at work. blue river was delighted for he loved the child nearly as much as chance he. since the day of silence's reappearance aunt cinnamon spent more and more time down at blue river's cabin and this just gave her another excuse, not that one was needed. so there was another pair of eyes to watch and still more love for chance to bask in.

without a doubt chance's favorite activity in the world was sitting among blue river's statues. although less than a year old, aunt cinnamon first notices whenever among blue's river angels chance would sit perfectly still for very long periods of time. quite at home, he seemed to belong among the angels.

aunt cinnamon is led to comment,

-sittin' there the way he is now, chance look just like one of them statues...

blue river had to admit that indeed he did. not just only in his stillness but among the sculptures chance shared almost a familial resemblance to many of the faces.

-and to be able to sit so still... very unusual in a child so young. most times they's rippin' and runnin' and you has to be chasin' along behind them. after they start walkin' you usually can't even keep up.

everyone agreed.

-right peculiar.

as is the nature of babies, in what seems no time at all chance's third and fourth birthdays arrive and soon his fifth one quickly on its' way. folks prepare to celebrate it even though dance had not planned a party this year. one is quickly arranged by the deacon board which decides to hold it in the backyard of the church as it provided ample room and a central location. chance's birthday had become a town holiday.

it seems that as the light around chance grows there is less and less attention available to be paid to the twins and it suits them just fine. over the summer passage begins working in the quarry and is rarely home. what with time locked up in her room and chance spending most of his day with aunt cinnamon and blue river, no one notices silence quietly growing into womanhood.

well that is not exactly true, there is ba'y bruh and he notices silence plenty. ba'y bruh gets to church early so as to be sure to get an aisle seat. ba'y bruh spends his week in anticipation of watching silence's buttocks hitting the sides of her dress as she delivers her weight down the aisle to their assigned family pew and silence notices him too. it's hard not to, ba'y bruh is everywhere she turns it seems. lately he had taken to arriving at church with little gifts he hides during service, then furtively hands silence during the gathering in the church's front yard directly after service.

this sunday though ba'y bruh carries nothing in his hands and does not speak nor acknowledge silence in any way. instead he stands at the foot of the church steps and waits for dance to finish talking with the reverend falcon at which point ba'y bruh steps up to dance, offers his hand and in a firm voice speaks,

> -afternoon mr. dance. my name be elbert samuel patterson but everybody 'round here just calls me ba'y bruh. would like your permission to escort silence home after church on sundays, sir... if that would be all right with you?

ba'y bruh's request takes dance by surprise but as he thinks about it and turns to see the look in her eyes, dance realizes indeed silence has reached the age of courting. dance looks at this skinny, black boy standing formally in front of him. ba'y bruh's posture had not wavered as he stands erect awaiting dance's response. dance decides he likes him and appreciates the respect ba'y bruh attempts to demonstrate by coming to him in this manner.

> -assumin' that this is agreeable to silence as well...

silence nods, her eyes on the ground,

> -can see no reason why you can't accompany silence home.

dance admits to a jumble of mixed emotions as he watches silence and her beau stroll ahead of them. he faced the fact that although he had never given it any conscious energy, he thought because of her silence, she would marry late or not at all. watching the two of them walking in front of him dance is reminded, as all fathers of daughters are, that one day some man will replace you. silence was growing up and dance witnessing this passage right before his eyes.

passage also watches ba'y bruh and his sister ahead. he too could not quite understand what it is he was feeling. he did not like it, this feeling nor did he much care for this ba'y bruh. what he felt passage would not have been able to put into words but it made him edgy, tense and uncomfortable. the emotion passage is unable to identify was jealousy.

the more time passes the more permanent a fixture ba'y bruh becomes around the house. he is eventually invited to sunday dinner and takes to walking silence home from school. ba'y bruh seems as much at home in silence's house as he must have been in his own. chance had really taken to him as well. even time manages to be civil, though she makes no bones about the fact she is against silence courting this young. never-the-less silence and ba'y bruh grow inseparable and the closer silence grows to ba'y bruh the more sullen and withdrawn passage becomes.

as is the path of nature silence and ba'y bruh begin to need to explore one another. passage takes to spying on the young lovers as they attempt to find ways and places to be alone together, not an easy task. at first passage takes great delight in accidentally interrupting silence and ba'y bruh at just some critical juncture in their abortive attempts at exploration as often as he could. lately though he gets quite an erotic joy out of watching the two of them make out and passage becomes a voyeur. he is surprised at the power of his erotic ardor. after watching a particularly hot petting scene in the barn he finds himself kneading his man-flesh while thinking of the softness of his sister's breasts and when he dares to imagine the magic down which grew between her legs the magnitude of successive ejaculations that always follow nearly cripple him. he wants to feel that softness. passage becomes obsessed. no amount of reasoning any longer makes sense, she is all he can think about. he smells silence everywhere. there was nothing passage could do, he could not remove silence from his mind.

passage begins to dream of silence in the night where she would come to him naked, all wet with desire. after a particularly hard night he awakens to find himself soaked and his member throbbing with the pain of such a massive erection that passage makes a decision. all social mores and religious injunctions against it be damned, virgin passage vowed to know that hidden softness even if it was the last thing that he did.

at that moment passage begins to plot silence's demise and with it his own damnation.

※

forty eight

in the path of silence

silence is waited for by ba'y bruh. women decide the time of intimacy. keepers of the guard, they define its' boundaries. aunt cinnamon's wisdom on that subject simply,

> -a man chases a woman until she catches him.

for silence it is time. she decides on the night of the harvest moon. she knows there will be celebrations as people bring in their major crops for the season. it was also the night of chance's birthday party. so caught up is silence in anticipating ba'y bruh that she doesn't hear the warning signal that is her brother.

passage too is waiting for his chance at silence. somehow passage catches wind of silence's thoughts one afternoon and suddenly knows it will have to be soon. he watches and keeps close ties not only on silence's whereabouts but also a sharp lookout for ba'y bruh. he bides his time. passage moves into a dark space.

the weather the night before the harvest celebration changes quickly from threatening to ominous. silence decides she and ba'y bruh would consummate their relationship upstairs in the hay loft of the old barn. hardly anyone ever came there anymore, it served mostly as storage, holding any overflow of seed. there is no need for anyone to go there in the evening time at all. the plan was ba'y bruh would make his way over to the barn as soon after sundown as he could. silence would do the same. over the last two days she slowly and slyly deposited items she thought necessary for the evening, a blanket, soap and bucket of water.

silence spends the afternoon frying chicken, deviling eggs and making a valiant attempt at aunt affection's lemon pound cake which she has to admit is not bad for only her second try. the pound cake looks perfect yet lacks something. once again silence finds herself believing there is some special ingredient missing from the recipe that she had not been given. silence's domestic delicacies and culinary flights are not lost on her brother who discovers her hidden stash in the barn. although she is cooking for the celebration on the church grounds, passage perceives a greater purpose. they would all be away from the house. he sensed silence planned to give herself to ba'y bruh tonight. passage decides that urgency demand he take silence before ba'y bruh could spoil her.

as the sun sets passage finds himself nearly dizzy with anticipation. it is silence who is first to arrive at the barn. no one is in the house, they even get time to go out to the party. silence hears something when she enters the barn and thinks it ba'y bruh who is not having so easy a time escaping. he has been sent on a soda and ice run that is beginning to take on nightmarish proportions. now at their third store, they are still unable to find any rc cola or ice. as the colors from the sunset stretch further and further across the sky ba'y bruh finds himself more and more anxious, his mind on silence as hers' is on him.

a naked passage with a totally erect endowment hiding in the hayloft is not what silence expected to find. she barely has time to fully comprehend what passage's presence here meant when he springs at her. before she knows it silence is in the fight of her life, for as determined as passage is in achieving penetration, silence, once she comprehends what destruction passage is attempting to wreck, is equally determined he will not succeed but the element of surprise proves too detrimental and silence just a little too slow. passage is an animal. he knocks his sister to the floor face down and rips her underwear from her body. passage takes silence savagely from behind. penetration is an out of body experience. disbelief, betrayal and the tearing of trust are but the early emotions that filter to the surface initially before silence grasps onto rage, revenge and hate which are quickly to follow and remain the longest.

passage calculated every second, rhyme and reason up until the act but had not given one thought as to what reaction he could expect afterwards. at the moment of penetration silence releases a guttural admittance similar to the cry of a stabbed wolf, loud and sustained. despite himself, passage found it gave him great pleasure. in this life, his perverted lust has had little chance to exhibit itself and passage now finds himself so totally immersed in it as he approaches his release, he does not hear dance enter the barn or climb the stairs to see passage's naked behind in the midst of raping his sister who continues fighting against his every thrust.

when dance looks around at the celebration and finds silence missing, his second sight nudges him. chance is on aunt cinnamon's lap, where he has taken residence, playing hand games with blue river. dance locates time sitting talking with bernice over by the tables with the food. his eyes search the entire backyard of the church but there is no silence. after checking inside he realizes he can't find that skinny patterson boy either. something tells dance to double back to the house which is why he hears silence's horrid sound and follows it up to the hay loft and the tragedy that awaited him there.

passage is literally in the process of shooting sperm when dance's massive hands reach around his throat and lifts him up off of his sister. looking down and seeing silence lying there bloody, taken, wet with the pollution of her brother and her own waste which uncontrollably released as she fought to defend herself, deeply disturbs dance. in silence's frightened doe eyes that fleetingly search for escape in floor corners and on the ceiling, dance sees the eyes of freedom, remembers the soldiers and his own humiliation before something deep inside of dance finally shatters. there is a terrible rushing in his head as dance tumbles down towards irreparable damnation.

-so you want to hurt somebody? answer me boy! you the big man...

and right there in front of silence and god, dance, in what seems like the actions of a madman calmly forces passage to the floor. while holding him down with his knee and with one arm he pulls down passage's pants with the other. dance slowly removes himself from the restraints of his own pants, mumbling under his breath,

-so you the big man? wanna hurt somebody?

and with no ceremony, lubricant or kindness of any kind, delivers his own brand of old-time justice. as dance viciously enters, ripping his son he keeps repeating under his breath,

-so you want to hurt somebody?... well, how it feel?

and as he continues to ram himself harder and harder into his son he repeats,

-well, how it feel?

suddenly before ejaculation he stops, looks down at himself, disengages, pulls up his pants, sits down, takes his head and his tortured soul into his hands and cries like a baby. dance could not have told what came over him any more than he could have stopped. after removing himself from the bloody haunches of his son, he found himself no less traumatized than silence who sits perfectly still watching or passage ashamed, who looks at dance with eyes flaring hatred, totally destroyed.

dance reconfirmed the haunting truth that rape is not a crime of passion but an act of violence. what dance witnessed today in his child and in himself truly frightened him. the three of them lay there for an indeterminate length of time. this was to be a defining moment in their lives. everything that they later recalled would always be seen as either before or after this event.

by the time ba'y bruh arrives at the barn there is no one there to greet him. he climbs up to the hay loft to wait as planned. the place shows signs of struggle and there is a nearly undetectable scent of recent passion and blood lingering. ba'y bruh climbs down and looks around. he listens. ba'y bruh thinks he hears sounds in the house every now and again in the distance, moaning but then when he stops to concentrate he would hear nothing. something was wrong. ba'y bruh crosses the front yard and walks up the steps of the porch. there is no answer when he knocks three times on the front door although he is sure that someone was home.

when dance hadn't returned and she could not find silence, time came on home. she passes ba'y bruh on her way and the look on his face makes her worry.

-evenin' ba'y bruh.

-evenin' miss time.

-you lookin' for silence? well ain't she to home?

-no ma'am it don't appear so, i knock but gets
no answer.

-she wasn't at the church grounds when i left.
that's strange...

time's voice trails off as she suddenly wonders if possibly silence is gone again.

-well when i see her be sure to tell her you was here
askin' for her...

in hind sight a disappearance would have been preferable.

✳

forty nine

in the path of silence

about that night nothing was ever said and an untreated wound will fester. silence refuses to think about that evening though she could not escape it. she withdraws from the world and whenever ba'y bruh stops by she refuses to see him. she gives the poor boy no reason. with hatred silence watches for passage.

dance watches silence over the next few weeks. she carries her pain in silence and the pain in silence grows. dance watches for passage's return. dance loves his son yet now knows he could never forget the image he holds of passage attacking his sister. dance knows as well that passage would never forgive him. dance is at a crossroads. he's never before lost control as he had done and it takes him back to the time when he wandered around outside his mind. as dance stands watching his second son play he searches for signs to assure himself that his mind is not about to go again.

passage takes to the woods to lick his wounds and heal. he cannot go home. he becomes as a ghost and would not be seen by anyone for months. that is with the exception of blue river who stumbles upon passage on one of his early morning walks three days after the double rape. passage was in very serious pain and could barely move. blue river asks no questions but the next morning passage discovers a pile of aloe palms which he knows are used as a salve in healing along with several pieces of dried fish and a loaf of baked bread. for the entire time passage spends in retreat in the woods, every few days there was a gift of some kind, mostly food, once a knife and a hook for fishing, a small pan and some matches, still another time a blanket. passage knows these are from blue river though he never sees him again during his self-imposed exile. passage builds a lean-to, fishes and eats off of the land as he had been taught. this could have been a time for reflection and healing, instead passage plots only revenge.

as is the way in nature, women who share the same house will eventually flow together. cycles pull one another, so it should have been time that first noticed silence's missed menses. instead time sleeps through it.

silence watches for passage and dance just watches. so then for the watchers it becomes a time of waiting. the only one untouched by the prolonged silence of anticipation is chance who plays in his continuing innocence with the grace of a five-year-old who, well into mastering a command of counting numbers up to a thousand has recently learned to write and spell his name. it is chance that takes their minds off troubles, with whom they let down their guard and play. chance could climb up on a lap, look you in the eyes and drive all worry away. whatever he asked could not be refused. with chance it was safe to love and they each gave in willingly.

for nature giving is natural but so is it within nature to take. revelations reveal themselves, some quickly as in a dream, some unfold like a rose petal or wings of the butterfly. so it was through chance that providence would reveal itself and show her true nature. it started one sunday at church. silence kept to herself, her head down she moved somewhat listlessly, almost as if sleep walking. she did not look up when she passed ba'y bruh, who sat on the edge of his aisle seat, his eyes fixed on the church door for the first sign of silence. yet she passes as if she had not seen him. aunt cinnamon catches a whiff of something when silence steps by her to sit in their pew.

ba'y bruh is in a terrible way. silence had left things at such a tenuous place. she has not looked at him since the night he climbed into the loft and waited alone. he could take silence ignoring him if he only knew why but since that night she acted as if he did not exist. anytime he goes to her house silence refuses to see him. ba'y bruh is completely devastated, he has done nothing wrong. he fights back tears several times during service.

aunt cinnamon stands at the end of the pew on the way out so that silence will have to walk right pass her. this time aunt cinnamon stops the girl with the pretense of looking at the stitch of silence's shawl but really it is to move close enough so she could get a good smell. by the time she lets go of the shawl there is not a doubt in aunt cinnamon's mind that her grand-niece is with child. she watches silence back down the aisle,

-well i'll be damned,

aunt cinnamon lets slip from her lips out loud before she catches herself.

-and you will be too, cussin' in the lord's house...
have mercy!

she hears in affection's voice. cinnamon had begun to do that a lot lately, hear her sister's voice in her head. usually it was accusatory in some way or another. cinnamon refused to answer. they haven't settled their score and she still is not speaking to her sister, dead or not. cinnamon is convinced that she will receive her apology in heaven and until then she'll wait.

-the heifer couldn't be ornery enough not to say she
sorry in heaven...

then a more frightening thought occurs,

-suppose affection wasn't in heaven?

despite herself, from that day on whenever cinnamon got

down on her knees to pray for herself she also prayed for the soul of her sister. whatever cinnamon felt for affection, she knew eternity would be a very long time without each other for company, even if they weren't speaking. all this she thinks in the time that it takes silence to walk the few steps to the door. aunt cinnamon's experienced eyes could already see places on silence's body that would soon fill out. she looks at her grand-niece again and knows,

-somethin's wrong,

not with the baby, with silence. it isn't until much later, at the end of sunday dinner, when it comes.

-in silence there was no joy.

in all the young expectant mothers aunt cinnamon has seen over the years there was fear, some scared to tell their mothers and almost always petrified to tell their fathers but they all had some excitement about the new life growing inside. in silence she felt nothing. that night as the family sat on the front porch to take in the beautiful sunset on this uncharacteristically warm early winter's night aunt cinnamon stayed in to dry the dishes and to talk with silence.

-babies come into this world when it's they time. don't seem to care much whether they mama or they daddy ready or not. when it come time ain't nothin' a woman can do but push the baby out. your mama and your daddy know?

silence shrugs her shoulders.

-how far gone are you?

silence holds up five fingers.

-five months, already! and your mama don't know?
some women, hmpff..

is all that aunt cinnamon can muster. how could time not
know, the child living right here in her house and if she does
why hasn't anything been said to the boy. aunt cinnamon
would have to have a serious talk with time and dance!
silence shakes her head and holds up five fingers again. this
time aunt cinnamon comprehends,

-oh, just five weeks.

aunt cinnamon takes a breath and releases a sigh of relief.

-well there ain't no such thing as a little pregnant.
this some kind of mess. does the boy know yet?

a stony glaze crosses silence's eyes and her face becomes
immobile. she turns her gaze inward and suddenly there is
no silence left for aunt cinnamon to question. she watches
her grand-niece turn to stone.

-is it that patterson boy, the one you've been keepin' time

with? he seem like a nice enough young fella. you told
him yet?

silence keeps her face still as a statue and continues to stare
inward. aunt cinnamon realizes that there is little more to
be gained this evening. blue river escorts her home before
sunset. there will be time another day.

✳

fifty

in the path of time

-**w**ake up! you lay there sleepin' while your house on fire. give me strength... baby girl do you hear me? get up from there and tend to your daughter!

that is all aunt cinnamon has to say the next morning when she arrives before breakfast to talk with her niece. time is still sleeping when aunt cinnamon rages into her room, throws open her windows and pulls the covers off. when time still clings to sleep aunt cinnamon calmly returns with a ladle of water and proceeds to pour it on her head.

-get out of bed you lazy heifer.

suddenly wet, time awakens.

-be waitin' for you downstairs.

aunt cinnamon turns and storms out of the room. in a few seconds time could hear pots and pans begin to rattle as her aunt starts breakfast. soon snatches of some hymn reach time as aunt cinnamon searches around for ingredients for dessert. she needs something to keep her hands occupied.

-this gonna be a long day and we gonna need all
our strength,

thinks aunt cinnamon aloud.

-lord, lord, lord... baby sista's baby girl is havin' a baby...

aunt cinnamon smiles in spite of herself. she has had the
entire night to get use to the idea of being a great grand-
aunt and she likes it. no matter the circumstances of getting
here, this be her great-grand...

aunt cinnamon begins to hum in earnest. before long the
smell of hot apple sauce and biscuits became more than
even time could stand and she stumbles down to a table
laden with grits, eggs and last night roasted chicken in new
gravy. chance and dance are already sitting at the table and
even silence manages to find her way to a chair. seeing her
family around the table, time is struck once again by the
absence of passage and the seeming lack of concern by
either his father or sister. aunt cinnamon looks around and
picks up on time's thought,

-where is passage? come to think of it haven't seen
that boy for weeks.

there is an unnatural silence at the table. dance shifts in his
seat and looks down at his plate. most notably aunt cinnamon notices silence stiffen at the mention of her brother's
name.

-must be out sowing some wild oats...

aunt cinnamon lets her voice trail off. so out of her range of imagination or comprehension, aunt cinnamon could never suspect the truth.

-more likely lickin' his wounds,

thinks dance to himself.

-well we have more important things to discuss anyway. silence gonna have a baby,

aunt cinnamon adds with little fanfare. in time there is surprise. dance turns toward silence. time and aunt cinnamon both see the look of horror come across his face that only silence understands.

-we can't help the way we gets here.

aunt cinnamon continues,

-this is god's garden and he plants wheresoever he pleases...

she looks around the table at the blank stares,

-i do declare... she ain't the first to have a baby and she won't be the last...

time gives no reply as she reaches for another biscuit. dance looks down into his plate. silence fights nausea at the smell of eggs and finds it necessary to run to the bathroom. dry heaves are the only thing heard through the quiet she leaves at the table until chance, as is the way of five-year-olds, tries out the new phase he's recently heard,

>-silence gonna have a baby...

he tries it in his mouth a second time,

>-silence gonna have a baby...

and while time continues to eat, dance silently begins to cry.

✳

fifty one

in the path of passage

wanting revenge sustains passage, filling every fiber of his being from his innermost core to the ends of the jagged new growth protruding from his chin. in the now three months since the night of the harvest celebration he is still fixated on how to hurt his father, to do the greatest damage. he wants to destroy dance as he had been destroyed. passage thinks hard on what dance loves the most. when the simple answer comes so easily one night as he sat alone in the darkness of his lean-to passage almost missed it.

-an eye for an eye...

there is a cessation of all physical pain as soon as the biblical passage dawns on him,

-a son for a son,

he whispers aloud.

-that's it!

passage allows his mind to think on dance's other son, chance as a portal he could cross. a plan is not yet formu-

lated but he has arrived at a means. passage is now determined to take his father's chance in exchange for what
dance had taken from him. the realization that the solution
he sought lay so simply within his grasp proves soul
satisfying. that night passage sleeps soundly for the first time
in weeks, satiated with the knowledge of certain revenge
and the silent joy which springs there from. for the first
time since the night of the violations passage dreams and for
the first time in years when he awakens passage believes he
dreamt with silence. they had done so as children effortless,
every night but had not shared many since silence had
undergone her womanhood changes.

in the dream passage stands outside of himself and watches.
it is a summer evening. there are fireflies. passage sees himself standing on the steps of the house. silence is sitting in
time's rocking chair holding a baby in her arms. silence has
tears running down her face and the baby is also crying.
suddenly there is a loud thunderclap followed by a tremendous bolt of lightning which lights up the sky and illumi-
nates the house. for a while he is blind. time passes as it
does in dreams and when passage could see again neither
silence nor the baby are anywhere to be found. just as suddenly passage wakes and sits up. he remembers every detail
and in this way passage first catches glimpse of his unborn
child.

✳

fifty two

in the path of passage

    -the ever present will of god is the unknown factor,

the reverend falcon preaches,

        -it is this which we see as the random aspect of life,
    that which we call luck or chance. when a mother dies
    in childbirth or when god decides to call the most gentle
    baby to glory, how many times do we question why? in
    the end there must be a begrudging acceptance of the
    fact that about certain occurrences there is never
    understandin'. it is the lord's way and it is by faith
            in him we rise.

ba'y bruh sits nursing his mason jar of white lightning as he
muses over this morning's sermon. within his growing
intoxication he thinks of the reverend falcon's words as just
a way to justify all the bad that happens in life. ba'y bruh
has been sitting in the same spot at the little road house
shack since church where he found himself behind miss rita
and miss fannie elizabeth, holding her three-month-old son
on her lap, his nineteen, seventeen, fifteen, eleven, nine,
seven, five and three year old brothers sitting between their
father and uncle, whichever one was which. ba'y bruh was

paying the women no mind, his eyes trained on the door as he watched for silence. it had been five months since the night of the failed rendezvous. in all the time since he had not been able to get close enough to silence to do more than speak in passing. he only catches glimpses of her during sunday services. ba'y bruh was watching silence walk in with her grand-aunt and her father, his son chance at his side, when the wind blew open her coat and ba'y bruh caught the unmistakable pouch of pregnancy. he sat back, not wanting to accept what he saw. ba'y bruh, unable to believe his own eyes, apparently was not the only one to notice because immediately miss rita turned to miss fannie elizabeth and exclaimed,

-told you so and not a sign of miss time!

-well i do declare...

-look about four or five months gone to me.

-no wonder her mama don't show her face in the house of the lord.

-no not miss time.

-miss high and mighty, well she sure brought down a notch now!

sniggers miss fannie elizabeth in a voice which suggests that she doesn't care who hears it.

-well who the daddy?

-don't know. heard talk it's her own father,

whispers rita, conspiratorially. fannie elizabeth raises an eyebrow,

-that just plain nasty. dance? oh no, this is just too good...

and the two women let their heads roll back and howl with laughter. their laughter cuts into the heart of ba'y bruh more than anything has before. he would have given them no thought at all except he had seen with his own eyes. the image of the brown coat catching the wind and pressing the white dress against the outline of silence's expanding belly played over and over in ba'y bruh's mind allowing him no peace. the absent father gossiped about should be he.

-the innocents, they become angels,

preached the reverend falcon.

-so what of the guilty, do they become demons?

sulks ba'y bruh, his initial sense of betrayal replaced by disgust and anger. these keep him company as he sits drinking alone for hours at the back corner table that ironically dance

chose in his time of separation and it is to these emotions
ba'y bruh directs his question. as he sits there ba'y bruh
attempts to reconstruct a chronology that brings all he
knows into abeyance while making some sort of sense out
of this shadowy place he finds himself in. as the white lightning rushes through his blood the words of miss rita and
miss fannie elizabeth run again through his mind,

-well who the daddy?

-don't know. heard talk it's her own father.

he tried to study dance during service. he watched his face
as they walked up the aisle trying to understand a scenario
that found dance a monster of new proportions and
still left silence the innocent victim, anything else was
unimaginable.

-be ever vigilant to the lord thy god. for we
know not the appointed time, neither the hour or the
day. only he knows and the truth belongs with the lord.
the one thing of which we are assured of is its' comin'.
death's arrival is always untimely or so people attempt to
convince themselves. folks say, cut down in the prime of
life... gone before one's time... or for a child delivered
before its' parent, you cry out that a father should not
have to look down upon his son... that for a mother
to bury her child is unforgivable... that for
this there could be no

forgiveness. yet you forget that the scriptures teach us
that god gave his only begotten son...

bay bruh downs another swallow.

-suffer the little children to come unto me, for surely i
am the kingdom of heaven. i am the way and the light
and no one comes to the father but thru me,

continues the reverend falcon, he is in rare form. little beads
of sweat begin to form at his temples. he pauses slightly to
find his white handkerchief and wipe his brow before continuing.

-for truly he is the great time keeper... the keeper of
all scores. from the smallest baby to the oldest of men.
his eye is on the sparrow... there is glory to be found in
paradise, my friend. so do not weep for the one who
reaches the distant shore but instead rejoice.

on cue the choir stands and begins to hum.

-know for a certainty that their time of sorrow has
passed for there is no sadness in glory time. hallelujah!
i say there is no sadness in glory time!

in my father's house oh, there are many mansions and i
have just gone to live in one. oh no, not in my time but
in your time, in your time, lord... wade in the water...

wade on into god's water. give yourself to god's water.
immerse yourself! submerge yourself! drown yourself in
god's water! god's gonna trouble the water! hallelujah!
god is gonna trouble the water! and god's will be done!...
let the congregation say amen.

reverend falcon turns to the choir and they begin to sing.
when all the events had been placed in order some would
recall reverend falcon's sermon that sunday before the
tragedy as strangely prophetic. truly the reverend falcon
could take little credit for prophecy, he had no revelation, no
visitation. he preached that sermon simply to try and ease
the burden of his wife bernice's heavy heart. this had been
her first sunday back. she had lost a third child less than two
weeks before and was taking it hard. as the choir sings the
reverend falcon turns to search for the eyes of his wife. they
are missing as indeed bernice is gone.

ba'y bruh looks up from his stupor to find the figure of passage in the doorway of the little road house shack. after getting a jar passage attempts to cross to the rear door and the
steps out back, where he has taken to sitting his evenings. it
is from here he watches the sunset and contemplates his
revenge. so lost in thought is passage that he passes ba'y
bruh's table without even noticing him. when ba'y bruh
speaks up, so compelling is his question that it brings passage out of his haze,

-is your father fuckin' your sista?

passage stops and turns toward the question. he realizes ba'y bruh is drunk. in the same moment passage realizes that he's never really had anything against ba'y bruh except for his interest in silence.

-is he the father of her baby?

passage hears the pain in ba'y bruh's voice, even as his own heart begins to race. had he heard right? passage can't help himself and

-baby?

slip from his lips before he could stop it. it is confirmation of his dream and with no consciousness he begins to smile. he is to be a father. passage processes this information. not only had silence conceived in their few moments in the barn but everyone must think dance fathered the child. it was a wonderful revenge.

passage refocuses on ba'y bruh and becomes aware of the look of disbelief and disgust covering ba'y bruh's face. involuntarily passage begins to laugh. at first the laugh is small enough to be contained around the table but it grows to encompass the entire shack. passage can't help himself, he just laughs and laughs and laughs. he looks at ba'y bruh and the testosterone of the competitor rises up. passage can't stop himself. between breaths, when he can finally form the words, passage manages to get out two sentences before becoming unintelligibly lost to laughter,

        -dance, he ain't the father... i am!

for some seconds ba'y bruh looks at passage incredulously and then through his white lightning stupor ba'y bruh manages to ask,

  -what is wrong with you? that your sista... what's wrong with you people? what the hell kind of people are you?

✳

fifty three

in the path of passage

where there is no god how can there be grace? and where there is no grace there can be no gain. sacrifice is god's pre-rogative. it is he who oversees our coming in and our going out, the waxing and the waning. there can be no indian summer until there is a frost and sometimes despite all efforts to seed, the season is hard, the frost early and there is no guarantee of harvest. after having been told that man is made in god's image what happens when grace is with-drawn?

passage stands at the rise in the road and watches his brother play. blue river chases chance who holds a purple heart wood angel with a tremendous wing span he had given him. from this distance passage could not tell but the angel looked so much like chance blue river had had little choice but to bring it to the child. chance is enthralled with his gift. in the magenta light of the setting sun passage is not the only one watching the silhouettes of the little boy child and the old man chase the flying angel. time also watches. awake from that morning of aunt cinnamon's anointment, she has become vigilant.

-kinda like closin' the barn door after the horse is way off
down in the damn field, eh?

cinnamon can hear affection's voice in her head. time watched her silence grow bigger over the last six months. there is something in the swelling of silence that signals defeat in time. somehow she feels deeply this failure which her daughter carries in her belly. time is wounded that silence had not come to her and that in search of power, time slept when her child had needed her most.

time blames herself for this upcoming abomination, for she had not protected silence from her own father. yes, time over time too began to believe dance fathered this child. when informed he didn't seem surprised, did nothing and there was no demonstration of anger. he showed no inclination to have a conversation with ba'y bruh who should by all rights have been the first suspect. time found it incomprehensible she could have so misjudged dance but then as she watched his bastard playing in her yard she began to question just how far under the dance spell she must have been to have allowed things to reach this point. time is disgusted with her life, her husband and most of all with herself. once such a proud woman, time now found no desire to be seen in town. feeling herself the focus of gleeful gossip, she couldn't remember the last time she graced the doorway of the church. time refused the pitying eyes that would fall upon her. she needed to be alone. this was easy, dance stayed away at work or spent his time with chance whom he picked up from blue river on his way home. quite often blue river would accompany dance and chance home to their shack at the edge of his land as he had done earlier today. the three of them would sit together some nights for hours out there until well into the dark.

silence stayed mostly to herself. she had taken to sitting most afternoons among the wildflowers near the wall where she first disappeared. what time could not get a handle on was what sort of participation silence played in all of this. in the end, whether a willing participant or a forced one, their child was still a child and dance still her father. as she watched the dance of joy between chance and blue river from her window, time carried non-deposited vengeance heavy in her soul.

silence watched for passage. she more than anyone knew her brother, he had to return. passage stands unnoticed but silence senses him there. even in the twilight shadows silence recognizes him and so too their baby for it chooses that moment to kick and for the first time silence feels her load move.

                    –so it is alive.

she knows then that she hates this growing parasite within her stomach and she hates passage for trapping his creature inside her.

in the mounting darkness it was becoming increasingly more difficult to see, the time of day when light plays tricks with your eyes. suddenly silence raises her hand and stopping everything, emits a sound higher than anyone had ever heard before. the ears of every dog within a mile radius shoot straight up in the air. silence points to passage's silhouette on the rise of the path. her eyes are aflame reflecting the brilliant final light of day and as the sun departs silence stands and continues screaming.

everything freezes as all eyes turn from silence to the lone figure atop the hill. realizing that it is his brother, chance breaks out in a frantic run, his arms open, screaming at the top of his lungs,

-passage! it's passage! my brother passage!

chance is not the only one for silence also starts to run as quickly as her swollen abdomen allows. silence's eyes are trained on her brother, her every muscle straining to reach her goal. her intention clear, to tear his face to shreds then wrap her fingers around his throat and squeeze until the demon spirit vacated. silence had not run over the last six months and grown quite unused to the balance her new body now required. silence stumbles then trips on the roots of the tree that dance had cut down. at the sound of silence's screams dance comes running out of the woodshed from where he is stacking firewood chopped that morning. he turns the corner of the shed and running towards silence sees a hand reach out from the root of the tree and pull silence down onto her stomach.

passage sees silence go down. he wants to turn and run away. that is his intention but some power holds him in place. instead of moving away he in turn scrambles down the path drawn toward the house and his fallen sister, passing the open arms of a disappointed chance who turns and follows confused.

from her window time hears silence scream, sees chance take off toward the rise and the silhouette that she recognizes as passage. when she sees silence fall time takes the stairs two at a time as she runs off the front porch toward her daughter.

silence hits her head on the stump. unconscious and bleeding heavily from her temple, dance is the first to reach her.

-is she breathin'?

screams a breathless time as she reaches dance and the lifeless body of her daughter.

-can't tell,

cries dance, unable to quiet his own breath enough to listen.

-yeah, she's breathin' but she out cold.

dance looks up to see the eyes of passage staring down at him. for a moment he is unable to say a word as he digests his son's presence here.

-go and get some water,

yells dance. he rips off his shirt and wads it to hold against the bleeding. he sits down and holds his daughter in his lap much as he had done time those many years before. as passage places the bucket next to him dance whispers,

-just look at your handiwork. look what you done done to your sista. don't know how you can show your face here?

dance attempts to ground himself as he applies pressure to the flowing wound. time begins to wipe the blood off silence's brow and clean her face. time hears what dance says but can't quite digest it all. before time can finish her thought silence's stomach begins to heave. time lets out a mournful cry,

-oh god, not yet. it's too early,

but cry all she like, silence's stomach told the story. silence had gone into premature labor.

-mr. blue, would you please go get...

time does not have to complete her request. blue river is

already on his way to fetch aunt cinnamon. he only makes it to the bend in the road when he confronts her shawled figure hurrying down the path toward her grand-niece. aunt cinnamon felt something in her bones when she heard those high pitched screams which set the dogs off howling. she grabbed her bag and hurried this way.

aunt cinnamon just reaches blue river when they hear the splash. dance has just about centered himself enough to begin to reach for the earth connection below when he hears the splash. passage stands transfixed when he hears the splash and occupied with silence, time is not even sure what she heard. it is just a splash, the kind of thud the bucket makes when it hits the center of the water in the well. it takes a moment to register to dance that the bucket lay on the ground next to him. terror strikes his heart and horror climbs across his face. he struggles to his feet and stumbles across the yard releasing an anguished cry as he calls out for his son,

-chance!... chance!!!!!

there is no response. dance reaches the open well. he calls out for his son once more,

-chance!!!!!

next a second splash is heard and then nothing as if the well had eaten father and son. then suddenly,

unbelieveably there is a third splash and turning aunt cinnamon does not see blue river.

-it was as tho' the whole world had lost its' mind, throwin'
itself down this well… and the well swallowin' up
people whole,

aunt cinnamon remembers saying.

there are relatively few moments of pure terror where in the
time between heartbeats one even forgets to breathe or that
time can bend, sometimes to breaking. the silence
following the three splashes was filled to brimming, laden
with abject, unabated horror concealing both life and death.

three souls go down into the well that night, none comes
back unchanged. one is saved, one is drowned and one
returns an angel.

✳

fifty four

in the path of blue river

an angel's miracle in the playground of time is only an angel's time in the playground of miracles and where grace demands it is always witnessed. watching blue river climb out of the well with chance was one such miracle, witnessed by aunt cinnamon, passage and time. so great a miracle that no one noticed at first blue river's clothes were completely dry or that no dance followed. it was only much later that folks questioned exactly how one could climb out of a well at all, much less carrying a child. aunt cinnamon focuses on the return of chance, time on silence who has not regained consciousness yet, her early labor proceeding. only passage keeps his eyes trained on the opening of the silent well where no second miracle occurs and no dance returns.

after assuring herself chance was alive, aunt cinnamon rises to cross to her grand-niece when her eyes fall on passage transfixed on the well. turning to look, she too finds no dance. cognition settles in and she looks at blue river who after putting down chance on the soft grass slowly turns and begins walking away. aunt cinnamon looks at his bone dry clothes from the back as he slowly carries himself down the hill and though she has never had any problems with her eyesight before, in the moonlit night she watches blue river fade away.

returning with each step, blue river comprehends more and more of what had occurred at the well. he can't fully accept it but he understands. it is a remembering, a consciousness returning, an awakening from years of a dream. in falling down the well his celestial nature took over and blue river remembered how to fly.

for a forgotten angel the path to finding misplaced grace can be terrifying. the road to remembrance laden with disbelief, non-acceptance and denial. to admit divinity in yourself is to glimpse its' absence in all those around you whom you live amongst and love. it is acceptance of the inherent and irrevocable differences between fire and clay. as an angel blue river remembered the sweetness of grace. his astral body refocused as the returned child of fire was once again recalled to the celestial realm.

✳

fifty five

in the path of dance

a late frost closes around sanctuary as a heavy mist rolls in hampering the men's recovery efforts. they work all night but it is still late morning before they are able to pull dance's lifeless body from the well. apparently he hit his head on the way down and broke his neck, death instantaneous. after having passed the night relatively well chance develops a high fever. bernice is called to watch over him. silence remains unconscious throughout her labor. she will do nothing to assist in the release of her despised affliction. at about noon silence unknowingly pushes a stillborn brown baby boy from her body. although she carried passage's incestuous seed, silence refused to birth the abomination or god give it life. despite all efforts the baby would not breathe. aunt cinnamon finally has to yield to nature.

-just too early... waren't ready for this world, not with the
burden he carried,

is all she could say when silence awakens later that after-noon.

-the truth is look like the baby just didn't want to
be born,

aunt cinnamon later confides to time,

-baby just refused to breathe.

passage was taking it all hard. when dance did not reappear out of the well something in passage broke. dropping to the ground, he lets out a sorrowful wail. he would revel in no revenge.

-no-oh! no-oh!, you bastard!

over and over again. heart wrenching sobs which fall upon deaf ears and hardened souls fortified by witnessing a miracle and coming within the sphere of grace. in this disastrous moment time stands still. staring at the tears in her son's eyes she begins to comprehend the destruction and chaos passage has wrought, a daughter/sister ruined, a son/grandson lost before birth, father/grandfather/husband, dead and his bastard in fever. a family torn asunder. time hardens. for the first time in her life she feels no compulsion to comfort her first born...

poison doesn't keep and eventually is carried by the tongues.

-now you know that dance's baby silence was carrying.

-uhm-hmm, silence done lost her daddy's child,

and folks fix their mouths to say,

> -surely it is for the best. it's god's will.

> -just plain nasty.

> -sin against god and nature.

-no tellin' what all monsters they be bringin' in here.

-forgive them father, for they know not what they do.

> -retribution is mine, saith the lord.

-the sins of the father are surely visited upon the son.

in this case the sins of which father visited upon which son? dance's sins lay upon passage surely and yet what visitation lay upon chance, the product of another sin. chance fell in the well, the only true witness to blue river's transformation. what of passage's sin visited upon his stillborn son? though the sin was popularly thought to belong to dance and by extension what visitation is brought down upon one's daughter?

the gossiping snakes drain their poisonous lies into one another's confidences, confirming their incorrect suspicions, blaming dance for passage's unforgivable sin, praising the wisdom of death in taking dance from amongst the living and returning him straight to hell, for there is no doubt in any mind that that is directly where dance was headed.

   -the devil got claim on that one for sure. god don't
   want him...

   -hmmm, hmmm, hmmm! and the devil might not have
   him either, shit... his own daughter! do jesus!

   -just goes to show how folks can fool ya...

   -never did like the black thing...

   -uhm-hmm... don't forget now he ain't from
   around here.

those same tongues hissed non-stop until the funeral planned for that next saturday morning.

in contrast there is little sound around the house as time prepares to bury her husband. for the last three days the house has been hushed as preparations were made. bernice and the sisters she deemed appropriate handle the household duties and the food dropped off by the caring and the inquisitive alike. aunt cinnamon cares for silence and time alternately. bernice looks after chance, he has been staying with her at the parsonage. he had not spoken since blue river returned him from the well. poor eyes stare unfocused at surrounding walls. his fever plays hide and seek with bernice and neither she nor passage leave his side. bernice finally coaxes him into a banana and honey sandwich and a cup of lemonade on which chance falls asleep before he can finish. he never wakes up. sometime during the night bernice goes in to check on chance and finds him dead. there is no explanation for his death. old folks claim dance came back for his orphaned son. it was decided that they would postpone dance's funeral another day and bury them both together.

that sunday morning as time arises with the sun she prepares to bury her husband and his bastard. she did not sleep but instead sat up the night before remembering their time together. dance had not been the best husband but she had loved him. he hurt her, there was no doubt but he as surely loved her as well. she recalled the quilt she created for him, it lined the box in which he lay. there was the night she first set eyes on him at the crossroads or the night before the lightning when they first made love. she glimpsed the look on his face as he carried her to the house just after she gave birth. time still has not had sufficient time to fully find and face her culpability in their life but she was awakening to its' existence. in the end time forgave dance most things because she was guilty of believing him capable of molesting silence when she herself had not seen the depravity within passage to whom she had given birth.

when time saw her son next at the wake she could barely look passage in the face. time had witnessed silence's screams. reclaiming her freedom in willing this act of early labor, silence spit passage's pollution out before time. in the triumphant look silence glared passage after awakening to find she delivered his underdeveloped seed too soon, passed between sister to brother all the hatred and consequentially all the love that ever would. silence never looked at passage again from that day, refusing to allow passage to take up any more room in her life. it wasn't that she ignored him, he simply did not exist.

when the family arrives at the little church house that over-cast afternoon it is packed. when news of chance's passing reaches the ears of the congregation folks stay after service. the town-folk turn out in force to bury their own. aunt cinnamon looks around searching for blue river among a sea of faces. there is no way he wouldn't show up for dance and chance's home-going ceremony. no one had seen him since he carried chance out of the well. she's looked every day but blue river was not to be found. he had simply vanished,

-into thin air,

she had been the last one to see him before he faded away. just as the family was about to walk in aunt cinnamon looks up to see blue river coming towards the little church, he carries the angel he last gave chance. aunt cinnamon takes a few steps in his direction to greet him as she locks arms with him. he is family and as much as anyone should be seated on the front row. blue river is in a bad way and so it is his muffled cry the congregation first hears as the doors open, even before the choir begins to sing.

dance is laid out nice. wrapped in time's quilt, dance truly gives the appearance of sleeping. they decide to bury chance in the same box lying next to his father, onto which blue river places his angel. time looks down on the body that had once housed the spirit of dance and understands completely the difference between spirit and earth. wherever dance is, he was no longer here and what lay before her were only his remains. time prayed for forgiveness for she still felt resentment even in her grief.

there in the same little church where the reverend hopkin's words had been said over dance and she nearly eighteen years ago now sat the remains of dance, who had been her life, her love, her trial and her burden. knowing how wrongly she accepted dance's guilt broke something inside of time. the reflection she caught of herself out the corner of her eye nearly blinded her. it was a weighted truth for time never learned of dance's taking of passage.

-it causes the mind to wander, it does at that... is there ever mercy? only god's mercy and his forgiveness... and is any death ever in vain?

begins the reverend falcon.

-could any life that god has deemed to put breath into

find its' completion in a vain-less death? without knowin'
the entire story, without seein' the entire board, which of
us is arrogant enough to second guess god? there is
never a question of too early or too late,
god is simply on time.

can i get a amen?

it's not always how we live, sometimes it's
how we die and nothin' became dance like his dyin'.
for what greater love is there than to lay down one's life
so that another might live? and then how much greater for
one's own son? dance died in the act of attemptin' to save
his son. unselfishly he gave up his life. how many
among us, if it came right down to it would have hurled
themselves down into that cold dark well? dance did so
with no hesitation. without thought or regard to self he
acted to save his son and within that great act of nobility
lies god's good grace, of that i am sure. now some of
you say to what purpose for here lies the son dance
died to save. was not his life given up in vain?
children who die in god's care are they not guaranteed
paradise? dance did not die in vain for in his death lay
god's good purpose, in dance's selfless act lies salvation.
this we should celebrate in his passin' and rejoice,
for in dance's dyin' he is sure to have been granted
the goodness of god's mercy.

dance and chance are buried in the small family cemetery

ihsan bracy

where time had gone into labor. no one notices the small grave near the base of the pear tree at the opposite end of the graveyard. there aunt cinnamon had taken the remains of silence's birth and buried him. he too was family. ironically thought silence while watching the heaviness in her mother's back as she followed her up the path towards the house, as much as time liked to dream, it was dance who first slept that final sleep. so lost in thought that she didn't notice when her mother stopped, silence almost runs into her before she sees what it is that's halts time. looking out towards the path that leads to the little graveyard stands dance, just as he had many times before, with his right hand cupping his forehead to keep the sinking sun out of his eyes.

-as big as life for everyone to see,

time was known to say later,

-like he escaped through the gates of hell,

added aunt cinnamon.

-then the light shifted and he was gone.

aunt cinnamon turns to say goodbye to blue river but he is nowhere to be found. she searches the tree line and catches a glimpse of his back as he walks into the woods. aunt cinnamon could have sworn she saw chance trailing behind him. the ground seemed to have no hold on the

311

souls lost, where the grace of god could not be found and when the love of a little boy for his savior angel was stronger than the passage of his time.

＊

fifty six

in the path of time

retribution is dangerous in the absence of grace and once granted, grace's loss is immeasurable. to be destitute of grace is to be abandoned into a joyless world, devoid of eternal essence. to be disconnected from grace is to suffer loneliness beyond comprehension, to continually wander in waste lands of non-existence, never again to see your likeness reflected anywhere. to walk in the absence of light which is its' unavoidable consequence, is to stumble sightless in half-lives and shadow worlds, void of all understanding, without direction. for the lost, redemption only appears attainable, for damnation or salvation, the paths look remarkably similar and grace alone is the divider. avoidance remains improbable, acceptance achievable and preferable. the only remaining constant is the sustained turning of the wheel and or the passage of time.

the years slip away slowly. time without dance moves to a different tune. reclusive, refusing to see anyone including bernice, she takes to her bed. she barely tolerates aunt cinnamon's presence in the house. time refuses to leave her room and only eats a small cup of broth and one boiled egg a day which silence brings around noon. time is so rarely awake and so evil when awakened, silence takes to leaving the bowl by the side of her bed. silence returns for the bowl around the evening meal which she eats alone, cooking enough food for two.

passage spends his days working on the small farm he created out behind the hut that dance built and sometime later when the house is still, passage would come through and get a plate. silence never sees him. aunt cinnamon takes to coming over and sitting with silence in the afternoons and blue river would sometimes stop by with chance, who even as a spirit was still growing like a weed. it's during these visits that aunt cinnamon learns something of the children of fire and their world that exists so near by. blue river is a forgotten angel, something he discovered when he threw himself down the well. children of fire have the ability to take on the physical characteristics of children of clay but the danger apparently lies in remaining too long without returning to their natural state. of his celestial cognition, blue river remembers nothing since childhood until the night of the well.

aunt cinnamon doesn't question blue river any further and never again speaks on it outside of time's porch but has no doubt that chance's spirit survives. she could see him even now, playing with his angel in the yard when the light hit just right.

lulled by the stillness of an afternoon's passage, the isolated conversationalists sit on the porch sipping lemonade as time strokes. if she called no one heard. it is only after silence goes in to retrieve the bowl, finding it untouched and unable to drag time back to this shore of consciousness, that she finally discerns the paralysis on time's left side when in her dreaming comma she only opens her right eye.

power comes looking for silence but instead finds time. time had been dreaming, calling, needing to see the face of power once more before dying. he could not ignore her need. time does not cry out when she hears power call her name. kinder and gentler than the last time they met. she remembered the two of them as children, playing. time never knew of the celestial territory that lay so close to sanctuary or that she had waited for one of its' wandering angels. she never knew what laws had been broken with the joining of clay and fire in the bringing of silence to birth.

power gathers time in his arms holding her ever so tenderly. he holds her like that for years and in return time holds him powerless, for as much as there is no way for time to extricate herself from the grasp of power he also cannot release her. time holds power to protect silence for she knows he has come for their daughter and cannot until he is released. nothing will relax the paralysis of time's stroke.

time never again regains consciousness and takes no other nourishment in the remaining years other than the baby's bottle of vegetable broth that silence could sometimes get her to drink. before power would be released from her hold some eleven years later time dies, forever in his embrace.

✳

epilogue

in the path of silence

the evening before the funeral services silence finishes packing up all the belongings she would carry and closes up the house. by about three o'clock in the morning she is through. quietly she crosses to the kitchen drawer and removes the butcher's knife which she habitually sharpened for just this occasion.

without upsetting the stillness of the night silence furtively crosses the path to the woods and walks silently down off the hill to the small hut that dance had built on blue river's land. the night remains silent and silence carries herself with such a stillness not one of it's early morning secrets are disturbed.

the other worldly glow of her skin suddenly finds reflection in the moonlight which reappears just before she arrives at her brothers' doorstep. soundlessly silence slowly enters the cabin and with the intensity of radiance shining directly through the open window has no trouble finding her way to passages' bedside.

as silence stands above the sleeping figure she raises the meat cleaver high above her head and waits for her brother to look up. if only passage but opened his eyes silence had little doubt she could draw the blade down across his neck as she had done so many farm animals before. instead all he did was pass gas, turn over and smile.

in the end silence had not even enough love left to kill him, so when she finally brings down the blade it is only across passages' pillow, where it would remain until he woke.

after the burial service silence walks off the land forever and never in this world would brother or sister breathe the same fetid air again.

∗ ∗ ∗

END OF BOOK ONE

A graduate of Bennington College, Ihsan Bracy is a former member of the New

York State Council on the Arts and former chair of the Theatre Department of Talent Unlimited High School, NYC's second largest performing arts high school. Ihsan's major educational credits include directing five Manhattan, three NYC and a third place National Shakespeare Championship as well as an ARTS National Finalist in Theatre. A spoken word and Brooklyn based artist, Ihsan

ihsan bracy, photo by Neil A. Kaku

has performed all across the city including a long running appearance at The Triad as part of composer Michael Raye's Soul Gathering.

Paths of Sanctuary is author Ihsan Bracy's second work of fiction. His first book *ibo landing: an offering of short stories,* (Cool Grove Press, 1998) is currently being work-shopped by NYU in preparation for an upcoming Broadway run by The Mirror Repertory Company where Ihsan is the Arts and Education Coordinator. As Artistic Director and Founder of The Tribe Ensemble, a multi-ethnic theatre repertory company based out of the Jamaica Arts Center for thirteen years, Ihsan authored and directed *Against the Sun, the Southampton Slave Revolt of 1831.* Author of two volumes of poetry, *cadre* and the *ubangi files,* Ihsan has twice been a CAPS Finalist and is an elected member of the New Renaissance Writer's Guild. A former member of The Family (La Familia) Inc., his credits include prolonged theatre workshops at Bayview Correctional Facility for Women, the Spofford Home for Juveniles and Riker's Island, which culminated in a forty prison inner city tour. Ihsan directed Juan Shamsul Alam's *Benpires* which received a Pulitzer Prize nomination in theatre.

Author's acknowledgements

I first would like to give praises to the ancestors and the orishas. I would like to thank these voices for allowing me to hear. I would like to thank Islah for always taking care of me, Zakiyyah, Mustapha and Jihad for their continued support. A special shout out to Deborah, who listened no matter what, and to all my readers who gave me invaluable feedback. I love you all.

—ihsan

ihsan bracy's first published work of fiction:

ibo landing: an offering of short stories
ihsan bracy
"bracy belongs with the group of writers who since Zora Neale Hurston have strived to manifest African American literature as sacred texts and griotic literature as working literature.   It is a significant work from a significant voice, from whom I suspect the best is yet to come"
—Arthur Flowers, Author of *De Mojo Blues and Another Good Lovin Blues* for Black Books Review

"This treasure box takes us from their torturous crossing out of Africa to the shores of South Carolina; from their migration from the Southern United States to several northern cities."
—Brenda Connor-Bey, from the foreword

"ibo landing is a truly remarkable first novel and a masterpiece of its kind...another jewel that tells the story of our people"
—Margaret Johnson-Hodge author of A New Day

please visit
www.coolgrove.com
www.wordbridgefair.org

paths of sanctuary

ihsan bracy

paths of sanctuary